DISNEY
FAIRIES

Tinker Bell and Friends

Book 2

Rani & Vidia

PaRragon

Bath · New York · Singapore · Hong Kong · Cologne · Delhi · Melbourne

First published by Parragon in 2008
Parragon
Queen Street House
4 Queen Street
Bath BA1 1HE, UK

ISBN 978-1-4075-2207-4

Printed in UK

All About Fairies

IF YOU HEAD towards the second star on your right and fly straight on till morning, you'll come to Never Land, a magical island where mermaids play and children never grow up.

When you arrive, you might hear something like the tinkling of little bells. Follow that sound and you'll find Pixie Hollow, the secret heart of Never Land.

A great old maple tree grows in Pixie Hollow, and in it live hundreds of fairies and sparrow men. Some of them can do water magic, others can fly like the wind, and still others can speak to animals. You see, Pixie Hollow is the Never fairies' kingdom, and each fairy who lives there has a special, extraordinary talent.

Not far from the Home Tree, nestled in the branches of a hawthorn, is Mother Dove, the most magical creature of all. She sits on her egg, watching over the fairies, who in turn watch over her. For as long as Mother Dove's egg stays well and whole, no one in Never Land will ever grow old.

Once, Mother Dove's egg was broken. But we are not telling the story of the egg here. Now it is time for Rani's tale . . .

Rani
and the
Three
Treasures

WRITTEN BY
KIMBERLY MORRIS

ILLUSTRATED BY
THE DISNEY STORYBOOK ARTISTS

1

"OH, NO!"

Prilla held up her hand and let the water splash into her palm. "Rain! The day is ruined. Hurry, let's get back to the Home Tree before my wings get wet." She fanned her wings and began to lift off from the ground.

Rani took Prilla's hand and tugged her back. "Don't be silly," she said with a laugh. "Rainy days are just as much fun as sunny days."

Prilla frowned. "I don't see how. If your wings get wet, you can't fly. And if you can't fly, then . . . " Prilla broke off. "Oh, Rani. I'd fly backwards if I could. I forgot."

"Don't worry." Rani smiled. She knew her friend Prilla would never hurt her feelings on purpose. All fairies loved to fly. Rani was the only fairy in Pixie Hollow who couldn't.

But Rani wasn't unhappy. She was too full of life.

The rain began to fall faster. Prilla covered her face. She flinched as each heavy drop struck her.

But Rani was a water-talent fairy. To her, every raindrop felt like a kiss. Rani loved the water, and the water loved her.

"Watch this, Prilla!" Rani ran as fast as she could towards a puddle. She skidded into the puddle, and the water formed a geyser that lifted her up as if she were on a pedestal. It twirled her around. "Wheee!" Rani cried.

Prilla clapped her hands. "Rani! Can you make it do that for me?"

"Sure! Come on in," she urged.

Prilla lowered her head and ran splashing into the puddle, just as she had seen Rani do. Rani stretched her arms out to the water. It moved towards her like iron to a magnet. She threw her arms up like a conductor signalling an orchestra.

Voilà! The water created a second geyser that lifted Prilla into the air until she was level with Rani.

Rani laughed. "Now let's see-saw!" The twin water pedestals began to move. Up and down. Up and down. Prilla up. Rani down. Rani up. Prilla down.

Soon both the fairies were laughing so hard, they were in danger of falling off their water pedestals. "Water down,"

Rani commanded, lowering her arms.

The twin geysers gently subsided. Rani looked down at a shallow puddle spreading out before her feet. She leaned over and grasped the edges of the puddle with her hands. Then she pulled up a sheet of water as if it were a bolt of silvery silk.

She wrapped it around herself like

a shimmering cloak. The water gleamed and glittered. It reflected the trees, the sky and the astonished sparkle in Prilla's eyes.

"How beautiful!" Prilla gasped. "You look like a queen."

Rani held out her hands and quickly caught a raindrop. She held her hands over Prilla's head and let it drip through her fingers. Each droplet was like a tiny diamond. The drops stacked up on Prilla's head and formed a glittering water tiara.

"Now you need a dress to go with that tiara. Water sequins, I think." Rani pulled off her water cape and twirled it in the air. The silky sheet of water broke into a thousand silvery drops. They rained back down on Prilla, clinging to her arms, legs and torso. Within seconds, Prilla was covered in a sparkling gown of water sequins, complete with a long train.

Prilla took a hesitant step. She expected the watery gown and crown to immediately drip away. But when she moved, they moved with her.

"Rani, you are amazing!" said Prilla. "No wonder you love the water. Believe it or not, I hope it rains again – "

" – tomorrow?" Rani said with a laugh. She had a habit of finishing her friends' sentences for them. "I wish that every day. But rain is rare in Pixie Hollow."

"Wouldn't it be wonderful if you could make it rain whenever – "

" – I wanted? Yes! I can't imagine anything more fun." Rani turned her face up and watched the clouds drift away. It *would* be wonderful to make it rain whenever she wanted. In fact, Rani had been thinking about that for a long time.

Just then, Rani saw a small rain cloud trailing behind the other clouds. Its fluffy edges gleamed silver against the late afternoon sun.

If Rani wanted her own' personal rain cloud, that little cloud would be the perfect one. Rani pressed her lips together, thinking.

"I'm getting cold," Prilla said. She shook off her watery finery. "I'm going inside to dry off. I'll see you – "

" – later." Rani waved as Prilla walked back to the Home Tree, where the fairies lived.

Prilla was the only mainland-visiting clapping-talent fairy in Pixie Hollow. In a blink, she could transport herself to the mainland where Clumsies – that is, humans – lived and urge them to clap to show they believed in fairies.

Everyone in Pixie Hollow had been amazed and surprised to discover that Prilla had such an unusual talent. But after a very short time, they stopped being amazed and surprised and took it very much for granted. After all, why *wouldn't* a fairy have an unusual talent?

Never Land was an amazing and surprising place with more kinds of magic than anyone could ever understand or imagine. But it was their talents that made the fairies so special. A talent was a kind of magic. And Rani's water talent seemed to be getting stronger and stronger every day. Her relationship to water, and all things made from it, was becoming more personal.

Maybe it was because she couldn't fly. Maybe Rani took all the passion that the other fairies devoted to their flying and devoted it instead to her talent.

Rani watched the clouds disappear into the distance. The smallest one with the gleaming edges trailed behind. There was something Rani had wanted to try for a long time. Something that would test the power of her talent.

Now, Rani decided boldly. *Now is the time!*

2

RANI RACED UP the spiral stairs inside the trunk of the Home Tree. She ran down the hallway. Her room was located at the very end of one of the longest branches.

Once she was in her room, Rani hurried to the window. She parted the seaweed curtains and peered out.

Rani's room was always damp, which was exactly how she liked it. A permanent leak in the ceiling dripped into a tub made from a human-sized thimble. A Never minnow swam happily in the tub.

Rani listened hard as the water splashed into the thimble. Water spoke a magic language full of dots, plops, plinks and gurgles. Rani felt as if the water were speaking directly to her. She could hear it encouraging her. It was telling her exactly how to coax the little grey rain cloud back to Pixie Hollow.

Rani fixed her gaze on the cloud and leaned out of the window as far as she dared. She stretched out her arms and began to imitate the sounds of the dots, plops, plinks and gurgles. She called out to the cloud, speaking the language of water.

The little cloud with the shining silver silhouette seemed to pause. Then, drawn by the sound of Rani's voice, it began to move towards her. While the rest of the clouds moved on, little by little the small cloud came drifting back towards the Home Tree.

Rani put every drop of her strength into her water spell. Finally, the cloud hovered right over the branch of the Home Tree where Rani's room was perched.

Exhausted, Rani sank back onto her bed. She listened to the rain patter on the ground outside. She felt the grey watery mist of the cloud come in through the window. It surrounded her like a soft, moist blanket. Her eyelids fluttered, and she fell asleep.

Rani awoke with a start. The sun shone on her face. She found herself looking out of the window at a clear blue sky.

"Why! I fell asleep in my clothes," she said.

She pulled the seaweed curtain aside and looked out at the sunny day. There wasn't a rain cloud in sight.

Rani realized that she had been dreaming. She couldn't help feeling disappointed. Having her own little rain cloud would have been wonderful.

She hurried downstairs. As she stepped outside to look for Brother Dove, she heard someone call to her.

"Yoo-hoo! Rani!"

Rani looked up. She saw Prilla waving from the window of her own room in the Home Tree.

Prilla flew out of the window and landed lightly on the ground beside Rani. "I had such a good time playing in the rain yesterday. I was almost disappointed when I woke up and saw – "

" – the sun?" Rani finished for her. "Me, too. In fact, you'll laugh when I tell you what I dreamed."

Rani told Prilla all about her dream. Prilla giggled at the idea of Rani having a cloud of her own. "What a shame it turned out to be a dream," she said. "But don't be too disappointed. Sunny days might not be as much fun as rainy days, but they're good for getting things done. What shall we do today?"

As they stood chatting in the soft, yellow

morning sunlight, a shadow slowly moved overhead. It blocked out the sun. Moments later, a raindrop splashed down next to them.

Rani looked up and drew in her breath. Hovering overhead was a small grey cloud.

"Prilla! It's the cloud from my dream!" Rani exclaimed.

"It can't be," Prilla said.

"It is!" Rani argued. "I know it. I feel it. It's my very own cloud. Oh, Prilla! It wasn't a dream. I am so lucky!"

Suddenly, Rani heard an odd sound. It sounded like laughter. But it also sounded like water moving through a pipe. "Did you hear that noise?" she asked Prilla.

"I heard a gurgling sound," Prilla replied.

Rani looked down and saw water collecting in a hole next to a root.

The water bounced around in the hollow, bubbling and frothing. "I guess that's what we heard." She turned her face up and spread her arms, welcoming the rain. "Just think," she said to Prilla. "Now I can take a walk in the rain every single day, and nobody else has to get wet."

Prilla flew a few feet to the side so she was out of the cloud's shadow. The drizzle fell only on Rani. Prilla laughed. "How perfect. Come on, let's walk to Havendish Stream and see if it follows."

The two fairies began walking towards the stream. All the while, the little rain cloud hovered over Rani and showered her. Some drops plopped on her head, as if the cloud were teasing her and trying to get her to join in a game. Rani broke into a run, trying to escape the drops. The little cloud chased her. It pounded the top of her head with water. Finally, she gave up and slowed down.

Soon Rani and Prilla were laughing so

hard they could hardly move. Once again, Rani heard the sound of strange laughter. This time it sounded like water rushing out of a tap into a copper pot.

Rani began to get an odd feeling. Someone – or something – was watching them. But who? What?

Then suddenly, out of the corner of her eye, Rani saw a figure zip from one flower to another.

Rani pretended not to see. And she didn't say anything to Prilla. She was already planning a way to catch the spy.

"Come on, Prilla," she said in a loud voice. "I'll race you to Havendish Stream." Rani broke into a run. Prilla chased behind her, flying a few inches overhead. Then, without warning, Rani came to a sudden stop and whirled around.

Prilla shot past her. "Hey!" she cried out in surprise.

Rani kept her eyes focused on one spot. Whoever it was, or whatever it was, froze. It stood perfectly still, hoping to blend into the background. But Rani's eyes were keen. "I see you," she said.

Rani heard a mischievous giggle. It sounded like a bucket splashing down into a well. "If you can see me, I guess there's no point in hiding," the strange creature said. It stepped forwards.

Prilla flew over and landed on the ground next to Rani. "What is it?" Prilla whispered.

It looked like a fairy, but it wasn't. For one thing, it had no wings. In fact, it had no body either. It was a transparent, shimmering figure made of clear water. When it stood still, it was almost invisible. But when it moved, its watery form reflected the sky, the trees and the flowers.

Rani stared at the remarkable creature.

"Who are you? And why are you following us?"

The watery figure laughed. The noise sounded like water splashing in a fountain.

"My name is Dab," the creature said. "I'm a water sprite. And that's my cloud."

"*Your* CLOUD!" Rani cried.

Dab nodded. "Yes. My cloud."

Rani was horrified. "Oh, dear. I didn't know it belonged to anyone. You can have it back. I would never have called it to me if I had known."

Dab laughed. It sounded like water swirling around a rock in a stream. "I've been following you," she said. "I wanted to see what kind of a cloud keeper you would be. You really have a way with rain clouds." Dab darted this way and that, reflecting colours like a prism. "Clouds are sensitive creatures.

You must be a very special water creature yourself." Rani blushed with pleasure. "Well, I am a water-talent fairy. That's why I was able to call the cloud. I guess it's also why I could see you when you were standing still."

She sighed. "I'll miss having my own cloud. It is such a treasure. I can't help feeling envious."

Dab shimmered. "Surely you fairies have treasures of your own?"

Rani laughed. "Oh, yes. Of course. But nothing as wonderful as a rain cloud."

"Maybe you would like to look after the cloud for me?" Dab suggested.

"You mean the cloud could stay?" Prilla asked, her eyes wide. She turned to Rani. "Wouldn't that be fantastic?"

Dab chuckled. It sounded like water pouring from a watering can. "Would you promise to be a good cloud keeper?" she asked Rani.

"Of course," Rani replied.

"Promise on your talent," Dab challenged.

"I promise on my talent," Rani

said promptly.

Dab smiled and shimmered. "Good! I now pronounce you the official cloud keeper. But there are a couple of things you should know. Clouds need a lot of attention. Someone must lead them and watch over them. Otherwise, they get nervous and fidgety. If they get riled up, they make a tremendous ruckus. Thunder. Lightning. Wind. Sleet. Hail. Even the little ones like that" – she pointed her transparent thumb towards the sky – "will make trouble if they get upset."

In the distance, Rani saw something in the sky. Lots of great, big, fat, fluffy, grey rain clouds moving in her direction.

"Ummm . . . " Rani pointed to the sky. "What are those?"

"The rest of my clouds," said Dab.

"Why are they coming this way?" Rani asked.

"Because you're the official cloud keeper now," Dab replied. "From now on, wherever you go, they go."

"I can't keep them all!" Rani cried.

Dab chuckled. "You have to. You promised. You promised on your talent."

"But . . . but . . . I thought I was promising to keep one. One small one."

"Where one goes, the others follow," Dab explained.

"You didn't tell me that," Rani protested angrily.

"You didn't ask."

"You tricked me," Rani accused.

Dab laughed. It sounded like water hammering on a tin roof. "Yes, I did. I've been keeping watch over those clouds for the longest time. I'll be glad to have a holiday."

"A holiday? What kind of a holiday?"

"I'd like to see Never Land in the sunshine.

When you travel with rain clouds, you never really get a good sense of the scenery. So I thought I would do a little sightseeing."

By now the entire sky was filled with dark grey clouds. A heavy rain began to fall. Rani had to shout to be heard over it. "But when will you be back?"

Dab laughed. "That depends on you."

"Me?"

Dab nodded. "You told me you have no treasure as wonderful as a rain cloud. But actually, the fairies of Pixie Hollow have three wonderful treasures – treasures that everyone would envy and want to possess. When you guess what those three treasures are, you must name them out loud and then say, 'I wish you back! I wish you back! I wish you back!' Until then . . . you're in charge."

And with that, Dab disappeared into the air.

It was a long, wet walk back to the Home Tree. Prilla's wings were so heavy with rain she couldn't get off the ground – not even with double sprinkles of fairy dust.

Rani looked up at the sky. The grey clouds hovered overhead. Sometimes they dropped gentle rain. Sometimes they dropped heavy rain. And sometimes they just contented themselves with being damp.

"What are we going to do now?" Prilla asked.

Rani noticed that Prilla had asked 'what are *we* going to do', and not 'what are you going to do'. She felt grateful that her friend wanted to help her.

"Well," Rani said, "I must say, I don't think Dab's riddle is very challenging. Pixie Hollow has lots of treasures. It shouldn't take us long to guess them. Mother Dove's egg is one." Mother Dove's egg was what kept the creatures in Never Land from growing old.

"What about Queen Clarion's crown?" Prilla suggested.

"Yes! That's two. Maybe Mother Dove is the third. Let's see if we're right." Rani lifted her voice. "Hear me, Dab, wherever you are. In the name of Pixie Hollow's three treasures – the blue egg, Mother Dove and Queen Clarion's crown – I wish you back . . . I wish you back . . . I wish you back!"

Rani and Prilla stood very still, waiting for Dab to appear.

But nothing happened except that a big, fat raindrop fell and splashed on Rani's head. "Okay," she chirped, refusing to worry. "It may be a little harder than I thought."

"We will figure it out," Prilla said.

In spite of the chilly rain, a wave of

happiness warmed Rani from head to toe. She was glad Prilla was such a good friend.

4

Two DAYS LATER, it was still raining. As Rani sat drinking tea, she couldn't help noticing that the tearoom was full of glum fairies.

Rani reached out and took a crumpet from the breadbasket. The crumpet bent slightly, then broke off. It landed with a plop right in her cup of tea.

Dulcie, who had baked the crumpets, sighed impatiently. "Every single piece of pastry is soggy. And there's nothing we can do about it with the weather so damp."

A laundry-talent fairy folded her arms over her chest. "We've got piles and piles of wet laundry. But we can't hang it out to dry until the rain stops."

"I don't understand it," said Iridessa, a light-talent fairy. "Usually Pixie Hollow only gets as much rain as it needs. But we've had a good bit more than we need. In fact, we're having too much. The roots of the Home Tree are so wet the fairies on the first floor are complaining of rising damp."

Rani said nothing. The first day of rain had been fun – at least for her and Prilla. The other fairies had seemed to enjoy the rainy day, too. Many had spent the time reading, chatting and tidying their work spaces.

But by the end of the second day, the mood had worsened. In the kitchen, the cooking and baking-talent fairies exchanged harsh words. The light-talent fairies were exhausted from trying to keep the hallways and workplaces lit. And the coiffure talents had given up in despair. In this kind of weather, they said, curls were impossible to tame. So they hung up a sign that read FAIRIES EXPERIENCING BAD HAIR ARE ADVISED TO WEAR A HAT UNTIL FURTHER NOTICE.

Rani listened to the unhappy voices. If the

other fairies ever found out that it was her fault the rain clouds were hanging around, it would be awful.

Prilla entered the tearoom and made her way over to Rani. "Any ideas?" she whispered.

Rani sighed. She had been racking her brains all night.

Kyto the dragon had a collection of rare objects far more priceless than anything in Pixie Hollow. Hook had chests full of pirate bounty, and the mermaids had the lovely treasures of the sea. What treasures did the fairies have that none of the others did?

Rani thought about her wings. She had asked Prilla to cut them off so she could swim in the ocean with the mermaids. It had been part of the quest to save Mother Dove and her blue egg.

As soon as she'd cut her wings off, they'd turned into tiny jewelled marvels. Those wings

– those treasures – had helped to save Never Land. Rani had given them to Kyto in exchange for his help.

Rani had never regretted giving away her wings – until now. Maybe the wings were one of the treasures Dab described.

Rani shook her head. No, that couldn't be it. Her wings weren't part of Pixie Hollow. They belonged to Kyto now.

It was clear to Rani that she and Prilla would have to go on a treasure hunt. But in the meantime, maybe there was a short-term solution.

Rani went outside and whistled for Brother Dove. He swooped down from a nearby branch. *Poor thing*, Rani thought. He was wet from head to toe.

"Maybe we can create a little dry time for

Pixie Hollow," Rani told Brother Dove. "The clouds will follow where we lead. So let's head for the caves and see if we can lose them there."

Brother Dove took to the sky and headed north. Rani looked behind her. Sure enough, here came the flock of grey rain clouds. They trailed at a distance, but they moved with steady purpose.

Rani indicated to Brother Dove that he should change direction. Brother Dove flew below the rain clouds and headed the opposite way.

"Faster," Rani urged. Brother Dove beat his wings harder.

Rani looked back and saw the clouds swiftly reverse their direction. They were determined to follow.

Then Rani spotted a cave in the side of a hill. "Let's hide and see what happens. Maybe they'll just drift away and find Dab on their own," she said.

Brother Dove dropped his altitude and soared below the hilltop. He circled once and then ducked into the mouth of a hidden cave.

Inside the cave, they waited. Rani peered out of the entrance at the sky. She could see the clouds, but she was hidden from them. The fluffy rain clouds began to mill around, bumping into one another like anxious, agitated sheep. They moved uncertainly this way and that. Within minutes, they were a tangled, rolling grey mass.

Thunder began to echo through the valley. It grew louder and louder, reverberating through the cave. Jagged lightning flashed. Rain poured down in sheets.

Rani peered out of the cave. The wind whipped her long hair in every direction. She grabbed on to a blade of grass to keep from blowing away.

This was terrible. She couldn't let it go on. If the clouds didn't calm down, they might cause another hurricane. *Besides*, Rani thought guiltily, *I promised I would be a good cloud keeper*. She had to honour that promise.

"Let's go," she told Brother Dove. He whisked her out of the cave. "Fly towards the rain clouds," she said. "But slowly. We don't want to spook them."

Brother Dove flew gently into the fluffy mass of clouds. The cloudy air was cold and wet on Rani's cheeks. Tiny bits of ice grazed her skin.

"I'm here," Rani said in a soothing voice. "I'm here. Everything is going to be fine." She reached out her hand to pat one of the clouds. Her hand sank into nothingness. But the clouds seemed to sense her presence. They calmed down.

"Come on," she said. "Let's go home."

The thunder began to die out. The lightning faded away. The hurling sheets of rain slowed to a light patter. Rani and Brother Dove flew back towards Pixie Hollow, the flock of rain clouds following behind them.

As they approached the Home Tree, Rani could see lots of fairies busy outside. They were gardening, dancing and hanging laundry out to dry.

They were not going to be happy to see the rain return. Nope. They were not going to be happy at all.

5

RANI LOOKED AT each and every one of the shells in her collection. Were there any treasures among them? Treasures that everyone would envy and want to possess?

Rani held her conch shell to her ear. She listened to the sound of the ocean. This shell was a treasure, but only to her. It had been a gift from the water fairy Silvermist. It was the first gift Rani had received when she arrived in Never Land.

There was a knock on the door, and Rani hurried to open it. Prilla stood on her doorstep. She wore a rain hat and coat made from a lily pad, and she carried a petal umbrella. Despite the fact that she was as cold and damp as the other fairies, Prilla had a big smile on her face. "Ready to search for treasure?"

"I'm ready," Rani replied. "First stop, Aiden's

crown repair shop. If there are any rare or precious jewels in Pixie Hollow, that will be the place to find them."

Aiden, the crown-repair sparrow man, was delighted to see Rani and Prilla. "Visitors! To what do I owe the pleasure?"

"We're taking inventory," Rani said quickly. "We're counting all of Pixie Hollow's treasures. Aside from Queen Clarion's crown, do you know of any extra-special jewels?"

Aiden rubbed his hands together. "You bet I do. Take a look at these." He reached for a wooden box and turned it upside down. Beautiful gemstones fell onto the table. They twinkled in the light.

Prilla gasped. "Oh, my! They are beautiful. Are they treasures?"

"Yes, of course," Aiden said. "Look at that

moonstone. It used to be the centrepiece of Queen Clarion's crown."

Rani reached down and picked up the moonstone. A tiny vein ran across it. "Is that a crack?" she asked.

Aiden nodded. "Yes, a wonderful crack. One day, Tink and Beck were flying with the Queen when a hawk came swooping down from out of nowhere."

Prilla gasped. "They could have been killed!"

"That's right," Aiden said. "But quick as lightning, Tink grabbed the crown from Queen Clarion's head. She took that dagger she always wears and pried this big moonstone right out of the crown. Then she threw the moonstone to Beck. Beck loaded it into her catapult and – pow! She got that old hawk right on his beak."

Rani and Prilla applauded.

"That hawk flew away and never came back. But the impact cracked the moonstone. Queen Clarion said never to fix it. That crack makes the moonstone priceless."

Aiden showed them every jewel in his workshop. He had a story to go with each one. It was almost an hour before Rani and Prilla left the crown-repair shop.

As they stepped outside, Prilla raised her umbrella. Her eyes were bright.

"Well? What do you think?" she asked breathlessly. "Did we find three treasures? Do you want to name them and wish Dab back?"

Rani sighed and shook her head. "Remember all the things we saw on our quest? Hook has bigger and finer jewels on his watch fob alone. Compared to his jewels, ours look like . . . well, pea gravel."

Prilla's face fell.

"All those jewels are treasures, but only to

us. They're treasures because of their history. But they're not treasures that everyone would envy or want to possess," Rani explained.

Prilla snapped her fingers. "I know! What about the pearls in the fountain? The beautiful pearls you brought from the Mermaid Lagoon."

Again, Rani shook her head. "Those pearls are nothing compared to the ones the mermaids wear. Their pearls are ten times the size of any pearl in Pixie Hollow."

"All right then," Prilla said. "Let's go and look at some art. Maybe we'll find a treasure or two in Bess's studio."

As they approached her studio, Rani and Prilla could hear Bess humming. They knocked on the door. Bess answered with a paintbrush in her hand.

When she saw Rani and Prilla, she grinned. "I'm so glad someone's come by. I have a new masterpiece to show."

"Is it a treasure?" Prilla blurted out.

Bess laughed. "Terence would think so." She stepped back and picked up a piece of sea glass on which she had painted a portrait of Tinker Bell. Light streaming through the sea glass made the painting glow.

Prilla clapped her hands in delight. "How beautiful!"

"Yes," Bess said. "I'm glad I had this nice piece of sea glass to practise on. Because – " Bess broke off. "Can you keep a secret?"

Rani and Prilla nodded.

"I have something wonderful. Something that will make everyone's eyes pop," Bess told them.

Prilla and Rani looked at each other. "Would you call it a treasure?" Prilla asked.

"Oh, yes. Look at this." Bess went to the corner where something very large was covered with a cloth. She removed the cloth with a flourish to reveal an enormous piece of sea glass. It was almost as big as Bess. "I'm going to paint a portrait of Mother Dove on it."

Rani's mouth fell open in amazement. "That piece of sea glass is huge. How did you carry it all the way from the beach?"

"Terence gave me a bit of extra fairy dust in exchange for painting that picture of Tink." Bess quickly covered the sea glass with the cloth. "Don't tell a soul about this," she begged. "I want it to be a surprise."

Rani and Prilla promised they would keep her secret.

Outside the studio, Prilla looked at Rani expectantly. "Well? What do you think?"

"It's a lovely piece of sea glass," Rani told her. "But I've seen pieces of sea glass much bigger and smoother."

Prilla's normally friendly face darkened. "Why are you being so discouraging about all of the treasures in Pixie Hollow?"

"I'm not!" Rani cried.

"Yes, you are," Prilla fumed. "You know what? I think you don't want to find Pixie Hollow's treasures. Because deep down you really want the rain to stay forever, even though it's making the rest of us miserable." And with that, Prilla burst into tears.

Rani felt tears forming in her own eyes. "Oh, no! Prilla! Why would you say such a thing? You must know that's not true."

Prilla cried harder. She pulled a leafkerchief from her pocket and dabbed at her eyes. "You're right. I *do* know it's not true. I don't have any idea why I said it."

"I know why you said it. You said it because the rain is making you cranky and sad, just like it's making everybody cranky and sad."

Rani handed Prilla her own leafkerchief, which wasn't much help. Rani's leafkerchiefs were always damp. She patted Prilla on the shoulder. "There, there," she said in a soothing tone. "There, there."

Then suddenly, Rani spied something. She pointed at it, so excited that all she could manage to say was, *"There! There!"*

6

IN THE DISTANCE, Rani spied a beautiful rainbow.

"That's it!" Prilla said happily. "There's always a treasure at the end of a rainbow. Maybe there's a treasure in Pixie Hollow we don't know about."

Rani nodded. "Brother Dove can fly to the top of the rainbow. We can follow it all the way to the end."

She whistled, and Brother Dove swooped down from a nearby branch. Rani hopped on his back. "Wish me luck, Prilla."

Brother Dove spread his wings. They flew high up into the clouds. All of Never Land spread out below them – the forests, the shores, the lakes, the streams and the villages. It was magnificent.

It might be lonely being the only fairy with

no wings, Rani reflected. *But I wouldn't trade places with anybody.* She might not have any wings, but no fairy could fly higher.

Up . . . up . . . up they went. They were heading for the rainbow's arch. Finally, they reached the place where white light bent in the mist and reflected all the colours. It was the highest point of the rainbow.

Brother Dove was breathing hard. His wings were losing strength. Luckily, he wouldn't have to fly any higher. Now they could glide back to the ground.

Brother Dove arced in the air. He began to follow the rainbow's curve back towards the ground.

Faster and faster they went. The ground seemed to rush towards them. Rani looked down and saw the roof of the fairy-dust mill.

"Aiiiiieeee!" she screamed.

As Brother Dove slowed, Rani pitched

forwards off his back. BANG! She fell right on top of the thatched roof. The thick straw cushioned her fall, but it was wet. Rani felt the roof give way beneath her.

CRASH! Rani fell through the roof. She landed with a *pooof!* right in the middle of a tub full of fairy dust. She flailed and struggled in the dust. Finally, Terence and Jerome leaned over the side of the tub and hauled her out.

Rani blinked her eyes, shaking the dust from her eyelashes. She saw the light fairies Fira, Iridessa and Luna. They stood with their hands on their hips, glaring at her. Nearby, Glory and Helios, two young light-talent fairies, burst into a fit of giggles.

But the other light fairies didn't seem amused at all. And Terence and Jerome looked perfectly horrified.

"Rani, what in Never Land are you doing?" Terence asked.

Rani had never been so embarrassed. "Well . . . I . . . um . . . saw the rainbow. And I thought I'd try to find out what was at the end of it."

Fira shook her head. "*We're* at the end of it. We light talents made the rainbow. And now you've ruined our work."

"We've been using light to try to keep the dust dry," Iridessa explained. "When our light mingled with the rain, it created a rainbow."

Rain began dripping through the hole in the roof. Drops splashed into the tub of fairy dust.

"Oh, no!" Jerome shouted. "You've punched a hole in the roof and now the dust is going to get drenched. As if we weren't having enough trouble keeping it dry already."

"Now, now," Terence said. "There's no time for blaming. Quick, get some oilcloth and cover the tubs."

Everyone sprang into action.

"Can I help?" Rani asked.

"I think you've done enough already," Fira snapped.

Rani felt her face flush hot and then cold with humiliation and regret. "Then I'll just, um . . . just . . . "

She couldn't finish. She ran outside, determined not to cause any more trouble.

But the moment she stepped outside the mill, a gust of wind hit her. It carried her up into the air.

"Help!" Rani cried. "Help!"

The fairy dust that covered her like flour had made her so buoyant that she floated. The tiniest puff of wind sent her tossing and turning through the sky like a leaf.

Rani had no wings, so she had no way to control her movements. She tumbled and rolled through the air, going higher and higher.

Soon she was lost in the thick fog of the clouds.

Tears ran down Rani's face. She had ruined everything. First, she had brought rain to Pixie Hollow. And now it looked as if she had spoiled Pixie Hollow's supply of fairy dust.

Another gust of wind sent her tumbling. She moved through the sky with the clouds. *Maybe this was the best thing that could have happened,* she thought miserably. *Maybe the clouds and I should blow away for good. Then Pixie Hollow can return to normal.*

Rani thought the other fairies were probably *glad* she had blown away. They would be relieved to be rid of such a troublemaker. And they would be especially happy to be rid of the never-ending rain.

Rani realized that none of those things were really true, but she couldn't help thinking them anyway. She felt miserable.

She began to sob. She was crying so loudly, she almost didn't hear her name.

"Raniiiii? Raniiiii? Where are youuuuu?"

Rani blinked her tears away. She peered through the foggy mist of the clouds. She couldn't believe her eyes. Here came Brother Dove with Prilla and Fira on his back. The two fairies carried long ropes of woven lemongrass looped over their shoulders.

Prilla unwound one of the ropes. "Tie one end around your belt, so we can take you down," she told Rani.

She threw the end of the rope to Rani. Rani reached out. But the motion sent her turning over and over.

"Try again!" Fira urged.

They threw the rope once more. This time, Rani managed to grab it. She tied the end to her belt. "I can't believe it. I thought you were going to leave me up here," she said.

Fira yelped, "Leave you up in the air? Rani! What are you thinking? Of course we wouldn't leave you."

Brother Dove, Prilla and Fira carefully towed her through the air, back to Pixie Hollow. As they approached the ground, Rani saw that several fairies had gathered. They peered up at Rani with worried faces. Queen Clarion was at the very front. Her helper fairies held broad petal umbrellas over her to keep her dry.

Fresh tears rolled down Rani's cheeks. But this time, they were tears of happiness. The fairies were all concerned about Rani. Despite the rain, they all had come to make sure she was okay.

As soon as Rani's feet touched the ground, the fairies began to applaud. Rani knew she owed them the truth. She held up her hands and took a deep breath. "I'm safe and sound.

And I have something to tell you all . . . "

Rani told Queen Clarion and the rest of the fairies the whole story of how she came to have the clouds and why they wouldn't leave.

When she was done, there was a long silence. Rani wondered what would happen next. Would Queen Clarion scold her? Banish her? Blame her for everything that had gone wrong?

Instead, Queen Clarion turned to the rest of the fairies and spoke in a clear, strong voice. "Fairies! You have all heard Rani. I know water sprites. They are mischievous, but they are not wicked. Dab will come back and take these clouds away. But she has posed a riddle and we must solve it."

The Queen waved her arms. "Let us all work together. Go to your rooms. Go to your workshops. Go to your studios. Look in your special hiding places. I want every talent group to bring their treasures to the fairy circle. We have so many treasures! Surely we can find three that everyone would envy and want to possess."

7

THE CARPENTER-TALENT fairies quickly raised tent poles in the fairy circle. The weaving-talent fairies brought their sturdiest cloth. Soon, a large canopy covered the entire clearing, protecting it from the rain.

Within an hour of Queen Clarion's announcement, the fairies and sparrow men began to arrive. They displayed their treasures on tables set up beneath the canopy.

Rani had never seen so many wonderful things in one place. The coiffure-talent fairies showed off hair ornaments and combs made from gold and pewter. The garden-talent fairies piled their table high with beautiful flowers and mouth-watering fruit. The table-setting-talent fairies brought out dishes made from porcelain as thin as paper.

"My goodness," Rani said to Prilla as they

wandered among the tables. "I didn't know we had so *many* delightful things in Pixie Hollow."

Tinker Bell's table gleamed with kettles, pans, and utensils. She held up a long-handled frying pan. "Have you ever seen anything more beautiful than the shape of that handle?" she said in a hushed tone.

Rani smiled and moved on. The fairy circle buzzed with activity as the fairies proudly displayed their treasures. Some had used balloon carriers to bring their offerings through the rain. But some treasures were small and easy to carry. The cooking-talent fairies didn't even need a whole table. Their most valuable things fitted into a little sandalwood box. Their treasures were recipe cards.

It was a wondrous bazaar. The dyeing-talent fairies displayed pots of dye in colours Rani had never even seen before. There were colours so rare they didn't even have a name. One of the dyeing-talent fairies showed her a small vial of vivid pink dye. It was nestled in a silk pouch in a golden box. "It's the only vial of Volcano Pink left in Never Land. This dye was made from the last sunset before the eruption on Torth Mountain."

Rani walked over to the mining-talent fairies' table. The only thing on display was an old pick. Orren, a mining-talent sparrow man, lifted it up. "She's a beauty, isn't she?"

Rani smiled. "Yes. But tell me about it. What makes it a treasure?"

"That's the pick that opened up the biggest vein of Never pewter ever found," he said proudly.

A group of art-talent fairies across the aisle scoffed at him. Bess said, "You're being silly, Orren. A pick isn't a treasure. A pick is a tool. A treasure is something like a painting or a sculpture."

At the next table, Queen Clarion's helpers laid out the Queen's favourite shoes, which were made from woven gold threads.

"Now who's being silly?" one of them said. "A treasure is something rare. You art-talent fairies turn out a dozen paintings a week. So how can they be treasures? Now *this* is a treasure." She held up a delicate piece of hand-made paper.

"What is that?" Rani asked.

"It's an invitation to a ball written in the Queen's own hand, using the royal pen. See? The ink is purple and it glitters."

Behind the Queen's helper, the sewing-talent fairies laughed. "An invitation! You think an invitation is a treasure? You're quite wrong. A treasure is something that takes time to create. Something that's made with skill and patience and creativity. Look around you. Every single fairy is wearing a beautiful, one-of-a-kind dress made especially for her. Any one of our dresses is more of a treasure than a pick or a painting or a pot or a note."

At this, the light-talent fairies rolled their eyes. "You sewing talents are so conceited," said Luna.

"We are not conceited," a sewing- talent fairy retorted. "If anyone is conceited, it's the light talents."

Fira, who was setting out a beautiful glow-worm lantern, scowled. "How dare you say that?"

"It's true," a passing music-talent fairy agreed. "You light talents always think you're the most important part of any party. You're always talking about how you have to rest and worrying about whether or not you'll have enough energy to glow. As if nothing else is important – not the food, not the dancing and certainly not the music!" The music-talent fairy angrily folded her prized trumpet flower under her arm and turned away.

Fira stamped her foot. "That's the meanest thing anybody has ever said. Maybe the light talents just don't need to come to any more parties."

"Maybe you don't," Dulcie said. "And maybe the music talents don't need to come either. Everybody knows the most important part of a party is the food. But to hear the sewing talents tell it, the only reason fairies go to parties is so they can dress up."

"Well, well, well," a sarcastic voice said. "What's all this quarrelling about?" The fast-flying fairy Vidia touched down in the midst of the arguing fairies.

"Vidia!" Rani exclaimed. "Have you brought your treasures?"

Vidia rolled her eyes. "No, dearest."

Rani suspected that Vidia's treasure was her secret stash of stolen fairy dust. Not that Vidia would admit it.

Vidia cast a scornful look around the fairy circle. "Let's face it, darlings, fairy dust is the only treasure worth having. Everything here is just a bunch of rubbish."

There were a number of outraged shrieks. Suddenly, the pent-up frustration from all the rainy days overflowed.

The sewing talents accused the laundry talents of deliberately washing their best dresses in hot water so that they shrank. The garden fairies complained that the animal-talent fairies didn't make one bit of effort to explain to the birds and squirrels why they shouldn't eat their berries. "From now on, don't ask us to coax the insects out of your gardens!" the furious animal talents replied.

That angered the cricket-whistling-talent fairies. After all, they said, they were often the ones who helped coax insects out of the gardens, not the animal fairies.

Soon, every single fairy was angry. Every single fairy felt unappreciated. Every single talent group was ready to take their treasures and go . . . when a terrible creaking noise brought them all up short.

Tink yelled, "Look at the canopy!"

Rani looked up. "Oh, no!"

While the fairies were arguing, the rain had collected on top of the canopy, causing it to sag. Before anyone could make a move, the entire canopy collapsed. Gallons of water and yards of wet cloth fell down, drenching all the fairies, along with their treasures, big and small.

8

RANI LOOKED AT the dismal mess. Broken tables, torn cloth, shattered pots, ripped garments, soggy paper, and muddy jewels were scattered everywhere. Every fairy was as upset as could be.

It was the rain that was making everyone so cranky and angry. It was the rain that was making everyone sad and gloomy. It was the rain that was ruining the peace and harmony of Pixie Hollow.

Rani whistled for Brother Dove. The faithful bird soared down. She climbed on his back.

"We're going to leave for a bit," she said. "What Pixie Hollow needs is some sunshine and some time to dry out, dry off and calm down."

Rani and Brother Dove took to the sky.

They circled around the clouds. Rani used the language of water – dots, plops, plinks and gurgles. She urged the clouds to move quickly.

Brother Dove carried Rani out of the clouds until she was in front of the flock. They flew low over Never Land, leading the rain clouds away from Pixie Hollow and towards the forest.

Rani looked down. She saw the leaves on the trees tremble as the raindrops fell. Some of the trees were a bit brown, she noticed. But after a splash of rain, they seemed to brighten and stand up straighter.

Rani smiled. It was nice to bring rain where it was wanted and needed.

Rani wondered if other parts of Never Land needed rain. She asked Brother Dove to fly higher so she could get a better view. To the south, she saw a yellow field that should have been green. "That way," she told Brother

Dove.

They flew over the field. Rani and Brother Dove let the clouds hover for hours, giving the field below a nice, long drink.

After they watered the field, they flew over a pond that seemed to be drying out. Rani and Brother Dove flew closer. The waterline was dangerously low. In a short time, there wouldn't be enough water in the pond to keep the fish alive.

So Rani and Brother Dove perched on a nearby tree limb and settled in for a long afternoon. The clouds hovered over the pond, slowly filling it.

As the water in the pond rose, fish jumped. The limp grass along the banks sprang up. Frogs leaped into the water, and schools of tadpoles skittered this way and that just below the surface.

Rani wondered where Dab was. Dab wasn't

a fairy, but she still had an important role to play. Every pond, field, garden and creature in Never Land depended on rain to stay alive. Herding and moving the rain clouds across Never Land was Dab's role. If she had been a fairy, it would have been her talent.

Even though Rani wasn't a cloud keeper, bringing rain where it was needed was a way of using her water talent. As Rani thought this, a wave of happiness warmed her from head to toe. It was a wonderful feeling.

"How could Dab abandon her talent?" Rani asked out loud.

"Wherever she is, it seems like she would be miserable."

Brother Dove made a noise in his throat. He pulled his wings in tighter.

Rani felt a pang of guilt. Poor Brother Dove. He wasn't a creature of the water, but he had spent the last three days soaked. She reached out and ran her hand down his wet feathers to show her gratitude.

Brother Dove cooed. Rani felt another wave of happiness as she thought of something she could do for him.

Tonight they would go back to the caves. Rani could sleep in the open, so the clouds would see her and stay calm. Brother Dove could sleep inside the cave where he would be warm and dry. She knew he would worry at first, but she would tell him to sleep well.

As long as I am using my talent to do something good, Rani thought, *I will be fine.*

That night, Rani lay on a ledge just outside one of the caves. She stared up into the dark, wet night. Her mind raced, trying every combination of Pixie Hollow treasures she could think of.

"*Hear me, Dab, wherever you are. In the name of Pixie Hollow's three treasures — a paper-*

thin porcelain tea set, Queen Clarion's handwritten invitation, and Orren's pick – I wish you back . . . I wish you back . . . I wish you back!

"Hear me, Dab, wherever you are. In the name of Pixie Hollow's three treasures – Dulcie's recipes, Bess's sea glass, and Vidia's fairy dust – I wish you back . . . I wish you back . . . I wish you back!

"Hear me, Dab, wherever you are. In the name of Pixie Hollow's three treasures – Lily's giant buttercups, Fira's glow-worm lantern, and Tink's frying pan – I wish you back . . . I wish you back . . . I wish you back!"

But nothing happened. Eventually, Rani's eyelids grew heavy and she fell sound asleep.

9

RANI AND BROTHER DOVE travelled around Never Land for four days. Everywhere they went they brought fields to life, restored health to ponds and made gardens bloom.

Rani always kept her eye out for Dab. Once or twice, she could have sworn she heard Dab's laughter. But if Dab the trickster was near, she had learned to move faster than Rani's eyes could see.

By the end of the fourth day, Rani and Brother Dove headed back to Pixie Hollow. Rani knew what she had to do, and she needed to tell the others.

As they approached Pixie Hollow, Rani could see that the fairy circle had been cleared of debris. Crisp, dry laundry hung from lines strung about the Home Tree. And the garden-talent fairies were tilling the moist soil to plant new seeds.

When they saw Rani coming with the clouds behind her, the fairies scrambled. The laundry-talent fairies plucked clothes off the lines as fast as they could. And the garden fairies darted indoors, dragging their baskets of seeds behind them.

Rani and Brother Dove landed. The fairies came out of their rooms and work spaces to greet them. They carried petal umbrellas and wore rain coats.

Prilla came running through the crowd with Tinker Bell close behind her. "You're back!" Prilla cried happily.

Tink pulled on her fringe. "You can't imagine how much we missed you," she said in a gruff voice. Rani knew it was the voice Tink used when she was about to cry but didn't want anybody to know.

The crowd parted, and Queen Clarion

hurried forward. Her helpers tried to keep pace with her and hold an umbrella over her head. But the Queen moved too fast. She didn't care about getting wet.

"Welcome. You have been missed," she told Rani.

"And I missed all of you," Rani said. "But as you can see, the clouds are still following me. I haven't figured out how to make them stop."

The entire population of Pixie Hollow groaned.

"But don't worry," Rani said quickly. "I'm not staying."

Everyone gasped.

"What do you mean? You can't leave," Prilla insisted. "You can't solve a problem by running away from it."

"I'm not running away," Rani protested. "But every part of Never Land needs rain eventually. Somebody has to keep these clouds moving and make sure that the rain gets where it needs to be. I guess that somebody is me."

"But what will we do without you?" Tink asked.

"I'll come back from time to time. When you need rain," Rani said. "But when you don't need rain, I'll be away."

Queen Clarion dabbed at her eyes with a gold-edged leafkerchief. "I fear that we have failed you. We have looked for treasure everywhere. And either we cannot find it, or we cannot agree on what it is."

Rani shook her head. "Don't feel bad. And don't worry. I'll be with the rain. As long as I can use my talent, I'll be fine."

Rani looked out at all the sad faces. Already, the rain was beginning to wilt their hairdos and dampen their wings. It was time to pack her things and go.

Twenty minutes later, Rani came out of the Home Tree. She carried a few spare tunics and her special conch shell tucked into a satchel.

Fira came rushing up. "The light talents have something for you to take." She placed a stone in Rani's hands. "It's a glow stone. It stores light during the day and glows in the night. It will give you comfort in the dark."

Rani was touched. After all the trouble she had caused, it was nice of Fira to worry about her.

A conducting-talent fairy lifted her hands, and all the music talents began to sing. It was the most cheerful melody Rani had ever heard. And it was so tuneful, she knew she would remember every note. "We wrote that especially for you," the conducting fairy told her.

"It's a song to sing when you're lonely." Rani was grateful. She knew the tune would come in handy.

Soon, every talent group was pressing something into her hands. A flint for starting a fire. A bit of extra fairy dust. A warm dress with a hood. Her favourite cookies.

Finally, Rani was ready to go. She was happy. She was content. And she felt brave and eager for adventure. But when she saw Prilla and Tink's faces, she thought her heart might break.

"Let's go, Brother Dove," she whispered. "Let's go quickly before we all start to cry." Rani didn't mind crying in front of the other fairies. She did it all the time. But she knew Tink hated for anyone to see her cry.

Brother Dove spread his wings. But before he and Rani could take off, Tink came running towards them. "Wait!" she shouted. "Wait!"

Brother Dove lowered his wings.

"I'm going with you," Tink said, panting. "To keep you company."

"But you can't stand being wet," Rani argued.

"I'll just have to get used to it. Besides, it's not forever. We'll be back in a few weeks because Pixie Hollow will need the rain."

"That's right," Prilla said. "And when you leave the next time, I'll go with you."

"We'll take turns!" Fira cried. "So you'll never be without a friend while you're away."

Rani began to cry. She had never been so touched. Yes, having a talent was wonderful. But she realized now that without friendship, life would be very lonely.

Another wave of happiness warmed Rani from head to toe. "Okay, Tink," she said. "Get your gear and let's go. It will be fun."

At that moment, Beck came flying rapidly

towards them. "Wait! Wait! Mother Dove wants to see Rani before she leaves!"

10

"Now, TELL ME everything from start to finish," Mother Dove instructed. She settled herself on her blue egg and fixed Rani with a kindly eye.

Rani sat down on the edge of Mother Dove's nest. She told her the whole story. She ended with a sigh. "I'd fly backwards if I could, but I can't. I can only fly forwards. So that's what I'm going to do. I just hope you'll forgive me for causing so much trouble."

Mother Dove's feathers ruffled. "Rani, my dear, that's why I wanted you to come. So that I could tell you this myself. No matter what you've done, no matter where you are, I will love you."

Another wave of warm happiness washed through Rani from head to toe.

"I would tell most fairies setting out on an

adventure to stay safe and stay dry." Mother Dove chuckled. "But to you, I will just say *stay safe and stay happy*."

"I *am* happy," Rani said gaily. "Isn't that odd? This should be the saddest day of my life. But I don't feel a bit sorry. In fact, I've never been so happy."

Mother Dove moved her wings a bit. "Oh? Why do you think that is?"

Rani thought hard. "Well, I guess because it's impossible to be unhappy when you know you have talent, friendship and love. What more could you want? What more could you need? As long as you have those three things you . . . " Rani broke off. Her mouth fell open. Her eyes widened.

Mother Dove said nothing, but her own eyes twinkled.

Rani drew in her breath with a gasp. "Oh, Mother Dove," she whispered. "That's it, isn't it?"

Mother Dove chuckled.

"I've done it, haven't I? I've guessed the three treasures."

"There is only one way to find out," Mother Dove said.

Rani lifted her face and called out as loudly as she could: *"Hear me, Dab, wherever you are. In the name of Pixie Hollow's three treasures – talent, friendship, and love – I wish you back . . . I wish you back . . . I wish you back!"*

A huge clap of thunder shook the nest. It was followed by the sound of water pouring over a waterfall. Dab's bubbling laughter filled the air. And in a flash, she appeared, as shimmering as ever.

"Well!" she exclaimed. "I was beginning to give up on you. I can't believe you took so long to figure it out. Maybe fairies aren't as clever as I thought."

Rani laughed so hard that tears rolled down her cheeks. "I was looking for *things*," she said.

Dab snorted. "Things! Who cares about things? Everybody has *things*. Those aren't the treasures everyone envies and wishes they possessed. Everyone knows that the fairies are happy. And they are happy because they have talent, friendship and love. So cherish your treasures, my friend. And don't make any more bargains with water sprites," she cautioned.

Dab darted from nest to bush, then from ground to sky. Rani heard her talking to her clouds in the magic language of water – full of dots, plops, plinks and gurgles.

Dab was gathering her clouds, calling them, herding them. Rani watched her work, admiring her bright quickness. Soon, the grey clouds were on the move.

Rani waved. But she didn't know if Dab waved back or not, because for the first time in days, the sun was shining in her eyes.

If there's one thing that every Never Fairy cares about it's looking good!

From **sassy** spider-web silks to *dazzling dandelion dresses* – they know all the tricks to make an outfit as original and stylish as possible.

To learn more about fabulous fairy fashions, read through this enchanting guide!

And remember … believing is just the beginning!

Fabulous Fairy Fashions.

Every new fairy arrives in **Never Land** wearing the remains of the first laugh that she was born from. But that is soon replaced once the **sewing-talent fairies** get involved!

Just like you, every fairy has her own style. There's no competition between fairies as to who looks the best – they each look great in their own way!

A fairy's dress sense is an expression of who she is – so every fairy and every outfit is original and unique. There are just so many fairy styles to choose from – **playful**, **thoughtful, colourful, dramatic, casual, smart** . . . the list is endless!

Fairies love creating beautiful, one-of-a-kind fairy outfits for both everyday wear and special occasions. Classy casual wear can be worn for daily tasks and playing games.

Sassy Shoes

When it comes to fairy footwear, the material
of choice is most definitely leaves!

Look at **Tink's** super-cute slip-ons! Made from
mint leaves and dandelion fluff, these shoes
are stylish and comfortable!

Knee-high ivy boots make a short sunflower
skirt look elegant and fun!

Lily pad flip-flops are great for water fairies when they're hanging out by the **bubbling** brook.

Soft moss slippers are perfect in the evenings when curling up in front of the fire and drinking warm buttermilk.

Fairy Flourishes

Whatever a fairy is wearing, you can bet she accessorises **colourfully** and **confidently!** A seed studded belt or a pink petal headscarf can enhance any outfit.

Fairies love to keep their heads warm in the winter with gorgeous hats and bonnets. Acorn caps, marigold head dresses and bouquet bonnets **look great!**

Garlands of daisy chains make fantastic necklaces or hairpieces.

Weave several strands of deep shaded ivy together and you can create a **stunning** belt to complement any high fashion gown.

Corsages are a fairy fashion **must-have!** Sunflower seeds, buttercup flowers or thistle blossoms work particularly well!

Take the Fairy Fashion Test!

Want to find out what your fairy fashion style would be? Take the test below to find out!

1. Which accessory can you simply not live without?
A. A sunhat
B. Your tool belt
C. Your leafkerchiefs
D. Your fairy dust pouch

2. If you could be anything other than a fairy, what would it be?
A. A bumblebee
B. A blacksmith
C. A mermaid
D. A star

3. What would your dream dress be?
A. A pretty flower
B. Something that jingled like a bell
C. Free and flowing like water
D. Something that glowed in the dark

4. Your favourite thing to do is?
A. Watch the grass grow
B. Eagerly await your next adventure
C. Swim
D. Soak up the sun's rays

5. You like your clothes to be?
A. Simple and sturdy
B. Short and green
C. Long and flowing
D. Bright and sunny

6. What are your favourite shoes to wear?
A. Wellington boots
B. Comfortable trainers
C. Flippers
D. Flip flops

Answers:
- *If you scored mostly As then you have garden fairy fashion style.*
- *If you scored mostly Bs then you have pots and kettles fairy fashion style.*
- *If you scored mostly Cs then you have water fairy fashion style.*
- *If you scored mostly Ds then you have light fairy fashion style.*

Vidia
and the
Fairy Crown

WRITTEN BY
LAURA DRISCOLL

1

EVERY FAIRY AND sparrow man in Pixie Hollow had received the same invitation. It was handwritten on linen in blackberry juice.

It was going to be the biggest celebration Pixie Hollow had seen in a long time. So, on the day of the party, the Home Tree was abuzz with activity. The Never fairies were busy getting ready to celebrate the Arrival Day of their beloved queen, Clarion, whose nickname was Ree.

In the kitchen, on the ground floor of the Home Tree, the cooking and baking-talent fairies were whipping up the seven-course royal Arrival Day dinner. The menu included dandelion leaves stuffed with rice, pine nuts and spices; oven-roasted mini-pumpkin soup; and pot-pies filled with dwarf mushrooms and mouse Brie. Dulcie, a baking-talent fairy, was churning out batch after batch of her speciality, the most delicious poppy puff rolls in all of Never Land. And for dessert, she made a ten-layer raspberry-vanilla cake with buttercream frosting.

Meanwhile, the polishing-talent fairies were hard at work in the Home Tree lobby and the dining hall. Every brass plate, every doorknob, mirror, window latch and marble floor tile was polished until the fairies could see their reflections just about everywhere they looked.

The decoration-talent fairies and the celebration-setup fairies zipped about the dining hall. They moved the tables and chairs. They draped the tables with gold tablecloths and delicate lacy spiderwebs. They sprinkled flower-petal confetti on every table and across the floor. They hung colourful balloons in the arched doorway.

The light-talent fairies did double duty. Some of them set up the firefly lanterns that would fill the room with thousands of dancing points of light. Others did a practice run of the light show they would perform for the Queen at the party. They skilfully flared and dimmed their fairy glows to create a dazzling display.

The sewing-talent fairies were putting the finishing touches to the Queen's dress. It was a full-length masterpiece of the finest silk, decorated with pale-pink rose petals, the softest green leaves and freshwater pearls.

Even Tinker Bell, a member of the pots-and-pans talent, was helping out. The cooking-talent fairies needed every pot and pan they could get their hands on. So Tinker Bell had risen early that morning. She finished mending all the broken pots in her workshop on the second floor of the Home Tree. Then she returned them all, making several trips between her workshop and the kitchen.

On her last trip down to the kitchen, Tink met up with her friend Rani, a water-talent fairy. Rani had been working in the kitchen all morning long. She was using her talent to help out with lots of little tasks, like getting the water to boil faster on the stove.

"Rani!" Tink called. "Do you have time for a break?"

Rani looked around the kitchen. Things seemed to be running smoothly. She didn't think she'd be missed if she stepped out for a few minutes.

"Yes," Rani replied. "I do have time. Let's go out and whistle for Brother Dove. Maybe he can fly us down to the beach."

Rani did not have wings, you see. She was the only Never fairy who didn't. She had given them up to save Mother Dove's egg –

and Pixie Hollow itself. Ever since then, Brother Dove had been her wings. Whenever she wanted or needed to fly somewhere, Rani just whistled for him, and Brother Dove came to her.

Tinker Bell and Rani left the kitchen through the back door. They stepped out into the late-morning sunshine. It was a glorious, clear day.

Tink took a deep breath of fresh air. "It's going to be a beautiful – "

" – evening," said Rani, finishing the thought. She had a habit of finishing others' sentences. "The perfect night for a party."

Just then, there was a rustling in the bush overhead. Both Tink and Rani jumped.

"Is it a hawk?" Rani cried in alarm. Hungry hawks were the greatest threats to the Never fairies' safety.

Instinctively, Tink flew in front of Rani,

shielding her. She strained her eyes and gazed up into the bush. She wanted to get a better look.

Then, as she made out the shape of a fairy among the leaves, Tinker Bell relaxed. She put her hands on her hips.

"That's no hawk," Tink said with a laugh. "It's Vidia."

A dark-haired fairy zipped down from above. She landed next to Tink and Rani. "Hello, darlings," Vidia said. She flashed them a sly smile. Vidia threw around words like 'darling', 'dear', and 'sweetheart'. But the way she said them made her fellow fairies wonder if she meant the opposite. "Why aren't you two inside getting ready for the big party – just like all the other good fairies? Hmm?" Vidia asked them.

"We were," Tinker Bell replied shortly. "We're – "

" – taking a break," said Rani.

"What's *your* excuse?" Tinker Bell asked Vidia.

Tinker Bell knew all too well that Vidia wouldn't be caught dead helping out that day. Vidia's relationship with Queen Ree was . . . complicated. In fact, Vidia's relationship with everyone in Pixie Hollow was complicated. She was the fastest of the fast-flying-talent fairies. But one day, Vidia had decided that being the fastest was not fast enough. Greedy for even more speed, she had done something cruel. She had plucked ten feathers from Mother Dove. Then she had ground those feathers into extra-powerful fairy dust that gave her extra flying speed.

After that, Queen Ree decided that Vidia couldn't be trusted around Mother Dove. She banned Vidia from Mother Dove's company.

Over time, Vidia had become more and more distant from the other fairies. She was the only fairy in Pixie Hollow who didn't live in the Home Tree. Instead, Vidia lived on her own in a sour-plum tree. Truthfully, most of the fairies and sparrow men thought that a little distance between them and Vidia was not a bad thing.

"Are you even *coming* to the party tonight?" Tinker Bell asked Vidia.

Vidia smiled. "To the Queen's party?" She laughed mockingly. "Of course not, dear. Why, that's what I'd call a waste of a perfectly good evening." Vidia paused and seemed to consider a new thought. "Oh, unless you need someone to fly in and snatch that gaudy crown off high-and-mighty Queen Ree's head," she said. "Now, *that* sounds like fun. In fact, that's quite a tempting idea – party or no party." Vidia shrugged. "Ah, well. You two dears have fun tonight!"

With that, Vidia took to the air. In a flash, she was gone.

Tinker Bell and Rani looked at each other and shook their heads.

That evening, as the sun inched its way towards the horizon, the activity in the Fairy Queen's chambers inside the Home Tree kicked into high gear. The Queen's four helper fairies – Cinda, Rhia, Lisel and Grace – were laying out the clothes, shoes and jewellery that Ree would wear to the party.

Lisel gently carried the Queen's beautiful new gown from the wardrobe and put it on the Queen's bed. She unbuttoned the five pearl buttons to make it easier to help the Queen dress later.

Grace picked out a pair of pointy-toed, rose-coloured silk heels for the Queen to wear. She placed them near the foot of the bed.

Rhia opened the Queen's jewellery box. She chose a pretty shell charm on a silver chain that went nicely with the Queen's dress.

Meanwhile, Cinda entered the Queen's sitting room and crossed to the crown cabinet on a side table. Naturally, the Queen would wear her crown to the party. Not only was it incredibly beautiful, but also, it was tradition for the Queen to wear the crown to any celebration. The crown was the most special fairy treasure in all of Pixie Hollow. Except for Mother Dove's egg, it was the only item that the fairies still had from the earliest days of the Never fairies. It had been passed down from fairy queen to fairy queen throughout the ages.

It was priceless and irreplaceable.

So when she opened the cabinet, Cinda froze.

The crown wasn't there.

2

WHEN QUEEN REE heard the news of the missing crown, she called an emergency meeting. Twenty-five message-talent fairies zipped out of the Home Tree. They fanned out in all directions to ask every fairy and sparrow man in Pixie Hollow to gather immediately in the Home Tree courtyard.

Queen Ree waited patiently. She watched as, by ones and twos and threes, fairies flew into the clearing. Many of them looked worried and whispered to one another nervously.

"What do you think is wrong?" whispered one fairy.

"It must be an emergency," whispered another, "or it wouldn't be called an emergency meeting."

"The Queen *does* look very serious,"

whispered a sparrow man.

They gathered in a wide circle around Ree. Some fairies hovered in midair. Some found standing room on the mossy ground. Some sat on toadstools or small pebbles. Everyone had his or her eyes fixed on the Queen, who waited silently as the crowd and the hubbub grew.

Soon the courtyard was bright with the glows of hundreds of Never fairies and sparrow men. Even Vidia was there. She lurked in the shadows of a mulberry bush. At last, when Ree judged that everyone was present, she cleared her throat. All of the fairies and sparrow men fell silent.

"Fairies! Sparrow men!" the Queen called out. "I have called this meeting to let you all know that there will be no celebration tonight."

A murmur arose from the crowd. The

fairies exchanged puzzled glances. No Arrival Day celebration? After all the planning and preparation?

"I need your help in finding my crown, which has gone missing today," the Queen went on. At that, the crowd's murmur became a cry of alarm. The crown . . . missing! Every Never fairy and sparrow man knew the crown's history. But what did this mean? What had happened to the crown?

"Do you mean that someone has *stolen* the crown?" Tink called out from her perch on a tree root.

"Now, now," said the Queen, trying to calm the crowd. "Let's not jump to any conclusions. There's probably a good explanation for why the crown isn't where it's supposed to be. And if we all work together, I'm sure we'll find it."

"Well, where was it last seen?" asked

Terence, a fairy-dust-talent sparrow man.

"Who was the last fairy to see it?" added Tink.

"How long has it been gone?" asked Iridessa, a light-talent fairy.

Queen Ree held up her hands to quiet the crowd. "Those are all good questions," she said. "Not all of them have answers yet. But maybe I should ask my helper fairy Cinda to come forward. She is the fairy who noticed that the crown was missing. After you hear what she has to say, you will know as much about all of this as I do."

Cinda sat with her talent in the front row of the ring of fairies. Her glow flared with embarrassment as she met the Queen's eyes. "Don't be afraid, dear," the Queen said. She waved Cinda over. "Just tell everyone what you told me."

Slowly, hesitantly, Cinda flew to the

centre of the courtyard and stood at the Queen's side.

"Well, there's not much to tell," she said quietly. She told everyone how shocked she'd been when she found the crown cabinet empty earlier that evening. "I thought maybe another fairy had beaten me to it – had already taken the crown out and laid it on the Queen's dressing table. But when I asked the others if they knew where the crown was, no one did!" Cinda looked up at the Queen. "We didn't know what to do! Nothing like this has ever happened before! So we told the Queen about it right away. She called the emergency meeting . . . and here we are."

Queen Ree smiled at her. "Thank you, Cinda," she said. Then, as Cinda retook her place in the circle of fairies, the Queen looked up at the crowd. "Now I have something to ask all of you," she said. "I would like you to think back over the last couple of days. Has anyone seen or heard or done anything that might have something to do with the missing crown?"

No one spoke for a long while. The fairies all looked expectantly around the circle. Their eyes darted this way and that, following the smallest noise – the slightest cough, rustle, or sigh – only to find that the fairy who made it didn't have anything to say after all.

Then, at last, a tiny voice piped up from a cluster of toadstools near the Home Tree front door.

"Queen Ree," said Florian, a grass-weaving fairy, "I saw the crown yesterday."

"You did?" the Queen replied excitedly. "Where? When?" Every fairy and sparrow man held his or her breath, waiting to hear Florian's reply.

"Well, you were wearing it," she said, "at

afternoon tea in the tearoom."

The crowd let out a sigh of disappointment.

"Yes, yes, Florian," snapped Vidia. "Who *didn't* see her wearing the crown yesterday at tea? That's not the kind of information we need."

The Queen turned to Vidia. "That's quite enough, Vidia," she scolded. "Florian was only trying to be helpful."

"Yeah, Vidia," said Rani. She hopped off her seat on a pebble and put her hands on her hips. "Besides, I remember you making a certain nasty comment about the crown this morning. What was it you said, exactly?"

Tink chimed in before Vidia could answer. "She said she was planning to fly into Queen Ree's party and snatch the crown off her head."

All eyes turned towards Vidia, who

crossed her arms and shifted her weight from one foot to the other. She scowled across the fairy circle at Rani and Tink.

"Well?" said Queen Ree, turning to look at Vidia. "Is that true? Did you say that, Vidia?"

"I said that I wasn't coming to the party," Vidia replied. "I think my exact words were 'unless, of course, you need someone to fly in and snatch that gaudy crown off high-and-mighty Queen Ree's head'."

The crowd gasped. To say such a thing – and right in front of the Queen herself! But then again, Vidia had never been one to mince words.

"That's not all," Tinker Bell said. "Then you said that the idea of snatching the crown sounded like fun – that it was something to consider – "

" – party or no party," said Rani, finishing

Tink's sentence. "It's true. She said that, too."

The crowd gasped again.

Vidia forced a laugh. "Oh, this is ridiculous," she said. "Yes, I said those things. But, really, what would I want with your crown, Ree? What would I do with it? It's not like I could steal it and then fly around wearing it, could I?"

Queen Ree looked troubled. "No, Vidia," she replied. "That doesn't make sense. Honestly, I have no idea what you would want with the crown. And honestly, I don't want to believe that you had anything to do with its disappearance. But these are serious charges."

The Queen looked around at all the fairies and sparrow men. "Does anyone else have any other information to share?" she asked. "Anything that might help us figure out this situation?"

Queen Ree and the crowd waited silently for several moments, but no one spoke. No one had anything to add.

"Well, then," the Queen said. She turned back to Vidia. "I have no choice. The crown is special to all of us. It doesn't belong to me. It belongs to Pixie Hollow. If we should find that anyone here has taken it, that would be very serious." She took a deep breath before continuing. "I think we would have to call it an act of treason," she said sadly. "And the only fitting punishment for such a crime . . . is lifetime banishment from Pixie Hollow."

Vidia's mouth dropped open in shock. "This is unbelievable!" she cried. "This is so unfair! Don't I even get a chance to defend myself? Can't I prove that I didn't do it?"

"Of course you can," Queen Ree replied. "But not tonight. It's late. We're all tired." The Queen took to the air. She hovered above the crowd. "Let's all gather again the day after tomorrow," she added. "We'll hold Vidia's hearing then, mid-morning. Everyone who wishes to come may do so. And, Vidia, you will have the chance to speak to the charges against you." Queen Ree nodded solemnly and brought the meeting to a close. "In the meantime, if anyone learns anything that might help us find the crown, please let me know. Thank you all for coming. Good night."

With that, the Queen flew off and inside the Home Tree.

One by one, the other fairies and sparrow men also flew away. Many of them, passing Vidia on their way out of the courtyard, shot her disgusted looks. Others avoided looking at her altogether.

3

VIDIA WAS STILL in shock. She sat on the ground in the shadows of a mulberry bush and stared blankly ahead of her. She made no move to go until it seemed she was all alone. Then, with a heavy sigh, she stood up and turned around – and saw Prilla sitting on a toadstool on the far side of the courtyard.

Kindhearted Prilla was one of the youngest Never fairies. She was fairly new to Pixie Hollow. She hadn't known Vidia as long as others had. But she had spent more time with Vidia than many of them. That was because Prilla, along with Vidia and Rani, had been chosen by Mother Dove to go on the great quest to save Mother Dove's egg. It hadn't been easy. Rani and Prilla had been forced to work with Vidia as a team for the good of Never Land. And in the end, they had succeeded.

Along the way, Prilla felt she had got to know Vidia a little better. Prilla knew why fairies thought Vidia was difficult. Sometimes she was nasty and selfish. She *had* plucked Mother Dove in order to get fresh feathers so she could fly faster. Vidia admitted that. But Prilla had seen another side of Vidia, too. Towards the end of the great quest, Vidia had had to make a choice: she could either share her extra-powerful fairy dust to save Never Land or keep it all for herself while the whole island lost its magic.

Vidia had chosen to share.

Maybe that was part of the reason Prilla stayed behind when the emergency meeting ended. Unlike some of the other fairies, Prilla didn't believe that Vidia was all bad.

"Vidia, are you okay?" Prilla asked. She

flew over and landed at the fast-flying fairy's side.

Vidia waved Prilla away. "Oh, save your pity, sweetheart," she replied. She forced a smile, but it quickly faded. "Do you think I'm worried? Well, think again. There's a reason I live on my own in the sour-plum tree. It's because I find all of you very irritating. What do I care if I'm banished from Pixie Hollow? I can't stand the place."

Prilla wasn't buying it. She could see the fear in Vidia's eyes. Oh, she knew that Vidia found Pixie Hollow annoying. But even Vidia wouldn't want to be forced to leave her home and live all alone, away from her own kind, forever.

"I'll help you, Vidia," Prilla offered. "Tomorrow, we'll start an investigation. We can ask around and see if we can find out what *really* happened to the crown. It's like a mystery that needs to be solved, don't you see?" Prilla jumped into the air and turned a somersault. "We'll be detectives!"

Vidia wrinkled her brow and looked sideways at Prilla. "Why do you want to help me?" she asked suspiciously. "And how do you know I *didn't* take the crown?"

Prilla landed and shrugged. "I don't know," she said. "Maybe you did take it. But I don't think so."

Vidia noticed that Prilla hadn't really answered her first question. "And *why* do you want to help me, dearest?" Vidia asked again.

Prilla thought it over for a moment. When she'd first arrived in Pixie Hollow, she'd had trouble figuring out what her talent was. Talents were a big deal. Fairies spent lots of time with the other members of their talent. They ate meals together. Their best friends were usually members of their talent. Without knowing what her talent was, Prilla had had a hard time finding her place in Pixie Hollow.

In the end, Prilla had learned that she was the first fairy with her particular talent – the first mainland-visiting clapping-talent fairy ever. There were no other members of her talent. But then other fairies had made her an honorary member of their talents. Over time, Prilla had settled into life in Pixie Hollow. She had made lots of new friends. She had found her place.

But she still remembered those early days.

Prilla looked Vidia in the eye. "I want to help you," she said, "because I remember what it's like to feel alone."

Vidia returned Prilla's gaze. For a long moment they stared at each other. Vidia never asked for help and she wasn't used to getting any. She wasn't sure what to say.

Vidia looked away. She cleared her throat. She looked up at the stars. She cleared her throat again.

"Okay," was all she said at last.

It was barely a whisper. But Prilla heard it, and she understood.

4

VIDIA AND PRILLA met after breakfast in the lobby of the Home Tree the next morning.

"Vidia!" Prilla exclaimed as the fast-flying fairy zipped through the front door. Prilla was eager to share with Vidia all the ideas she had for starting their investigation. She had come up with a list of fairies they could question and leads they could follow. "Vidia, I've been thinking – "

"Thinking?" Vidia said. She cut Prilla off and flew right past her. Prilla had to rush to catch up. "Now, why would you go and start experimenting with that?" Vidia asked snippily.

Clearly, Vidia wasn't going to be nice to Prilla just because Prilla had offered to help her. "Come on," Vidia barked. "We'll start by questioning the Queen's helper fairies."

Prilla struggled to keep up as she followed Vidia to the second floor of the Home Tree. They turned down the south-eastern hallway and soon flew up to the door of Room 10A, where Queen Ree lived.

Vidia knocked loudly on the door. When no one answered right away, she impatiently knocked again, more loudly.

Cinda opened the door. She peeked out into the hall.

"Ah, Cinda," said Vidia. She brushed past her into the Queen's sitting room without waiting to be invited in. "What a brave little fairy you were last night, darling – coming forward to tell your tale in front of that big, scary crowd." Vidia flashed Cinda a sickly sweet smile. "But we have just a few more questions to ask you and your fellow helper fairies. Don't we, Prilla?"

Prilla hadn't got any farther than the

doorway. She had never been inside the Queen's rooms before. She stood gazing at the elegant surroundings. The sitting room had pale peach walls, overstuffed sofas and a floral carpet. Beyond the sitting room were the sea-green walls of the Queen's bedroom. Prilla could see one corner of a large, high four-poster bed.

The three other helper fairies, Rhia, Lisel and Grace, flew out from the Queen's bedroom. They were carrying a pile of the softest spiderweb bed linen. They landed abruptly when they saw Vidia.

"What's *she* doing here?" Lisel asked Cinda with a sneer. Rhia and Grace also eyed Vidia warily. It was obvious that they thought she was guilty of stealing the crown.

Prilla flew forwards and tried to smooth things over. "We'd just like to ask you some questions about yesterday," she said hopefully, "so we can prepare Vidia's defence for tomorrow."

"*We?*" said Grace, her eyes wide with surprise. "Prilla, are you actually *helping* her?"

Prilla shrugged and her glow flared. "Yes," she replied. "There's no proof that Vidia took the crown."

"No proof *yet*," Lisel muttered under her breath. She turned away and led Grace, Rhia and Cinda over to a large table on the far side of the sitting room. They set the sheets and pillowcases on the table and began folding them.

"Listen, dearies," Vidia said. She flew across the room to hover over the helper fairies as they folded. "All I want to know is when each of you last saw the crown. It is your duty, as the Queen's helper fairies, to take care of all of her belongings, right? But perhaps in this case, you lost track of a certain something?

Perhaps you don't remember when you last saw the crown?"

The helper fairies' pride rose to Vidia's challenge.

"Of course we remember!" Grace protested. "The last time I saw the crown was the day before yesterday, in the evening. I put it back into the crown cabinet after Queen Ree wore it down to dinner."

Lisel nodded. "That's right," she said. She added a folded bedsheet to the growing pile. "I saw Grace put it away that evening. I was here in the room when she did it. That was the last time I saw the crown."

Cinda shook the wrinkles out of a pillowcase. "I saw the crown yesterday morning," she said. "Rhia took it out of the cabinet to make sure it was ready for the party. Right, Rhia?"

"Right," Rhia replied. "I took the crown

out and started to clean it. Then I noticed that there was a small dent in the metal." Rhia looked around at her fellow helper fairies. "Well, I didn't think it was right for the Queen to have a dent in her crown at her own party." The other fairies nodded. "So I took the crown up to the crown-repair workshop to have it fixed."

Vidia zipped excitedly to Rhia's side. "And when was this?" Vidia asked.

"Yesterday morning," Rhia said. She described how she had put the crown in its black velvet carrying pouch, taken it up to the crown-repair workshop and left it with Aidan, the crown-repair sparrow man. "I told him what needed to be fixed. I told him it was a rush. And I asked him to bring it back to the Queen's chambers when he had finished."

"I see," Vidia replied. "And he did? He brought it back?"

Rhia nodded confidently. "Yes," she said.

Then her brow wrinkled. "I mean, I think so." Her glow flared. "Well, actually, I don't know for *sure*."

The three other helper fairies stopped folding. They stared at Rhia. "Rhia," said Lisel in shock, "what do you mean you don't know for *sure?*"

"Well . . . I . . . I mean," Rhia stammered, "I told him I might not be here when he brought it back. I would be in and out. I told him he could leave it with any one of us, whoever was here." Rhia's eyes searched her friends' faces. "Didn't any of you see him bring it back yesterday?" she asked hopefully.

Lisel shook her head.

"Not me," said Grace.

"Me neither," said Cinda.

Rhia covered her mouth with her hand. It muffled the sound when she cried, "Oh, no!"

Prilla shot Vidia an 'aha!' look. "Well, if Rhia took the crown to Aidan," Prilla said, "and none of you saw the crown after that . . . "

Vidia zipped towards the door. "Come on, Prilla," she called behind her. "We have a crown-repair sparrow man to visit."

5

BY THE TIME Prilla caught up with Vidia on the fifth floor of the Home Tree, Vidia was already questioning Aidan in the crown-repair workshop.

"What do you mean, you didn't see the crown yesterday?" Vidia was shouting. She hovered over Aidan while he sat at his workbench. "Rhia said she brought it to you to be fixed!"

"I did!" exclaimed a voice behind Prilla. She turned to find Rhia standing in the doorway of the workshop. Prilla didn't realize that Rhia had followed her up from the Queen's rooms. She had wanted to hear Aidan's side of the story, too.

Aidan nervously scratched his ginger-coloured hair. He looked shocked. Moments before, he'd had his quiet workshop all to himself – as he did most days. Aidan's talent was a specialized one. There weren't many crowns in Pixie Hollow in need of repair. In fact, there weren't many crowns in Pixie Hollow at all! So most of Aidan's time was spent on his own, perfecting his crown-repair skills.

As a result of his lonely work, Aidan was quite shy. Even from far away, Vidia scared him. Now, suddenly, here she was, hovering over him and shouting.

"Please," said Aidan. He held up his hands in surrender. "I – I'm telling you the truth. I saw *Rhia* yesterday, but I d-didn't see the Queen's crown."

Rhia flew across the workshop and landed at Aidan's side. "Don't you remember?" she asked. She described again how she had come into the workshop on the previous day. She had asked Aidan to fix the dent in the crown, told him it was a rush, and left the crown there. "I asked you to bring it back to the Queen's chambers when you were done," she said. "So why didn't you?"

Aidan's big green eyes had grown wider as Rhia told her story. "Is *that* why you came into my workshop yesterday?" he asked her. "Rhia, when you came in yesterday, I had just finished doing some work with my gemstone drill." Aidan reached across his workbench. He picked up a tool that looked like a cross between a hand mixer and a screwdriver. "It works well, but it makes a terrible racket. Here, I'll show you."

Aidan took a piece of quartz from a pile of stones to his left. He aimed the drill bit into the quartz with one hand. He turned the drill's crank with the other. A deafening, high-pitched squeal filled the workshop. Vidia, Prilla and Rhia covered their ears with their hands.

"Stop, stop, stop!" Vidia shouted over

the noise. Aidan stopped drilling.

Prilla uncovered her ears. "Gosh, Aidan," she said. "How do you stand it?"

Aidan reached into the pockets of his baggy work trousers. "I use these," he replied, pulling his hands out of his pockets. He opened them to reveal several wads of dandelion fluff. Then he stuffed a wad in each ear to show how it worked.

"Let's cut to the chase," Vidia snapped impatiently. "What does all this have to do with the missing crown?"

"WHAT?" said Aidan loudly.

Vidia sighed and yanked the fluff out of his ears. "WHY DO I CARE ABOUT YOUR EARPLUGS?" she shouted.

Aidan shrank from Vidia. He turned towards Rhia instead. "Well, when you came in yesterday, I had my back to you. Didn't I?"

Rhia nodded.

"I still had the dandelion fluff in my ears," said Aidan, "because I was working with the drill." He shrugged. "So whatever you said, I didn't hear. When I turned and saw you standing in the doorway, I waved. Remember? But then you turned and left! So I figured you had just dropped by to say hello."

Rhia held her head in her hands. "And *I* thought you were waving to show that you had heard everything I'd said." She groaned. Then an idea came to her. "But whether you heard me or not, I *did* leave the crown here." She flew over to a tree-bark table near the door of the workshop. She pointed to a specific spot on the table. "It was in its black velvet carrying pouch. I put it right here." But there was no sign of the crown or the pouch anywhere on the table – just a jumble of scrap metal that Aidan had thrown into a pile.

"Well," said Prilla hopefully, "maybe it's

around here somewhere." She peeked under the table. Rhia checked inside some nearby cupboards.

But there was no crown or velvet pouch to be found.

Prilla sighed. "Aidan," she said, "did anyone else come into your workshop yesterday? Anyone besides Rhia?"

Aidan thought it over, then nodded. "Yes. Twire came by," he replied.

"Twire?" said Rhia. "The scrap-metal-recovery fairy?"

Aidan nodded again. He pointed to the pile of scrap metal on the table next to the door. "She picked up yesterday's scrap metal. She melts it down and recycles it."

Prilla gasped.

Rhia groaned.

Vidia pursed her lips and shook her head.

"What?" said Aidan.

Vidia flashed Aidan her sickly sweet smile. "Don't you see, pet?" she said. "If the crown was on that table next to the scrap metal when Twire came to pick it up . . . "

"She might have taken the crown away with the metal . . . " Rhia continued the thought.

Prilla gulped. "And melted it down!"

6

"FLY, VIDIA, FLY!" Prilla called out. And the fastest fast-flying-talent fairy in Pixie Hollow rocketed out of Aidan's workshop and zipped towards Twire's.

As she flew, Vidia wondered why she cared so much about saving the Queen's crown. *So what if I'm too late? So what if the hunk of junk has been melted down?* she thought. *What do I care? I've already got at least two other fairies I can link to the crown's disappearance – Rhia and Aidan.*

Surely Queen Ree would not banish her after hearing what Rhia and Aidan had to say.

Still, Vidia raced on towards Twire's workshop. She told herself it was because it would be easier to clear her name if she found the crown. But . . . was there a part of Vidia that actually *did* care about one of Pixie Hollow's oldest treasures?

Twire's scrap-metal workshop was on the third floor of the Home Tree. In her rush, Vidia barged through the door without knocking and flew straight into a set of metal wind chimes that hung from the ceiling.

Prrriiinnnnngggggg! The wind chimes rang forcefully as Vidia ploughed through them. Across the workshop, a startled Twire straightened up and took a break from her task – dropping bits of scrap aluminum and copper into a large vat of molten metal.

"Stop!" Vidia called out. "Stop what you're doing!"

Twire took off her sea-glass safety goggles and wiped them on her overalls. "What's the matter?" she replied in a calm tone, putting the goggles back on.

Twire was the type of fairy who always

saw the glass as half full. She found the hope in every situation – even the most dire – the same way she saw beauty in each piece of scrap metal, no matter how twisted or rusted. Twire had a passion for turning rubbish into beautiful items. They were all over her workshop: the wind chimes by the door, the flying-fairy mobile by the window, the lamp on the workbench. They were all crafted from scrap metal.

Twire also believed that most bad situations could be turned into good situations. So as Vidia began madly sorting through the pile of metal Twire was melting down, Twire tried to calm her.

"Whatever it is, Vidia, I'm happy to help. Just tell me what's going on," Twire offered.

Just then Prilla arrived, slightly out of breath. She watched as Vidia threw a piece of copper over her shoulder. It landed with a *clang* on the workshop floor. "The Queen's crown!" Vidia snapped. "Have you seen it?"

Twire shook her head. "No, Vidia. I haven't," she replied calmly. "What makes you think it's here?" She turned to Prilla. "Hello, Prilla," she said kindly. "Are you here with Vidia?"

Twire looked surprised when Prilla nodded, but she didn't say anything.

Vidia gave up her search and sighed an annoyed sigh. She impatiently repeated what Aidan had said: that Twire had picked up his scrap metal the day before.

Twire nodded. "That's right," she said. "I pick up Aidan's scrap metal every day. Yesterday I brought it back here, sorted it and began to melt some pieces down."

Prilla watched as Vidia leaned over Twire menacingly. "And you're sure you didn't find anything unusual mixed in with the metal?"

she asked. "Think carefully, love. The crown might have been in a black velvet pouch."

At this, Twire started. "Velvet?" she said, her face brightening. "Yes! Yes, I did find some velvet in the pile." She smiled and patted Vidia on the back. "You see," she said encouragingly, "we're on the right track. We'll figure this out."

"Oh, cut it out!" Vidia snapped impatiently. She shook Twire's hand off her back. "Just tell me what you did with it!"

Twire sighed. Vidia was a very negative fairy! Twire flew towards a tiny door in the wall at the far side of the workshop. Vidia and Prilla followed.

"Well, I didn't know it was a pouch," Twire explained as she flew. "I didn't feel anything inside it. But Queen Ree's crown is just about the lightest and most delicate thing ever made. That's probably why I thought it was a piece of unwanted fabric." Twire shrugged. "I was sure I could use it for something. But it had a few rust stains on it. You know, from being tossed around with the metal."

Twire pulled open a small, square door in the wall. It opened onto a metal chute that dropped down and away into total darkness. "I tossed it down the laundry chute with my other laundry," she said.

7

VIDIA TOOK OFF so suddenly that Prilla had to fly her fastest to catch up. So fast, in fact, that when Vidia paused for a moment on the Home Tree's central staircase between the third and second floors, Prilla bumped into her and fell over backwards.

"Oof!" Prilla cried.

"Watch where you're flying!" Vidia shouted. She threw Prilla a dirty look before flying on towards the first floor, where the laundry room was.

Prilla followed. "Well," she called after Vidia, "at least Twire didn't melt the crown down!"

"That's right," snapped Vidia over her shoulder. "She didn't melt it down. No such luck."

Prilla shook her head as she and Vidia

flew to the laundry room. At the bottom of the staircase, they turned down the hall that led to the kitchen. Then, dodging the cooking, baking, and dishwashing-talent fairies, they flew through the kitchen and into another hallway. At the far end was a swinging door with a small, round window.

Pushing through the door, Vidia and Prilla found themselves in the Home Tree laundry room. It was a huge room with towering fifteen-inch ceilings. The whitewashed walls and overhead lights made it seem like the brightest and cleanest room ever. Busy laundry-talent fairies and sparrow men flew this way and that. Some carried baskets of dirty laundry to the rows of washtubs, where other fairies were scrubbing away. Some pushed balloon carriers – carts kept aloft by fairy-dust-filled balloons – full of wet laundry. Still others stood before long tables, folding clean laundry.

Hundreds of laundry chutes carried laundry down to the laundry room floor from the workshops and bedrooms on the floors above. The dirty laundry fell into baskets. Each chute was marked with the floor number and room it came from.

Vidia and Prilla found the laundry chute labelled 3G. It was the chute that led down from Twire's workshop. A laundry fairy named Lympia was standing under it, sorting through some clothing in a basket. Prilla asked her if she had worked at the same chute the day before. When Lympia said yes, Vidia launched into her questioning.

"Did you find anything . . . *unusual* in Twire's laundry yesterday afternoon?" she asked pointedly.

"What do you mean, unusual?" Lympia replied. She eyed Vidia suspiciously. Like the Queen's helper fairies, Lympia didn't trust

Vidia. "Prilla, what's this all about?" she asked.

"We're on the trail of the missing crown," Prilla explained. She gave Lympia a rundown of what they had found out so far. She told her how Rhia had taken the crown to Aidan's workshop and how it had been accidentally picked up by Twire. And then how Twire had dropped it down her laundry chute without knowing it.

"Are you sure you didn't find a black velvet pouch mixed in with Twire's laundry yesterday?" Prilla asked Lympia.

Lympia started. "Oh!" she exclaimed. "Well, yes, I did find a velvet something-or-other. But what does that have to do with anything?"

Vidia sighed. "The crown was *inside* the pouch, precious," she said, sounding annoyed. "Honestly, if anyone had bothered to look inside the thing, I wouldn't be in this mess!"

Rolling her eyes at Vidia, Lympia turned again to Prilla. "I was going through Twire's laundry, sorting it into lights and darks," she explained. "When I found the piece of velvet, I put it aside. It couldn't be washed in the laundry, you see. It had to be cleaned specially."

Prilla nodded. That made sense. "So where did you put it?" Prilla asked.

There was a long pause as Lympia thought it over. "You know," she said at last, "I really couldn't say."

Vidia smirked. "Well, that's fine," she said in a falsely casual tone. She shrugged. "Tomorrow at my hearing, I'll just say that we traced the crown as far as the laundry room. But then we hit a dead end. Because Lympia *really couldn't say* where she had put Pixie Hollow's most prized possession!" Vidia turned as if to fly away. "This is a waste of time."

Lympia's glow flared. "No! Wait!" she called.

Vidia stopped in her tracks and turned around.

"Let me try to retrace my steps," Lympia suggested to Prilla. "Maybe that will help me remember what happened to the velvet pouch."

So Vidia and Prilla followed her to the balloon-carrier storage area. "Yesterday afternoon, after I sorted Twire's laundry, I picked up a balloon carrier and put the laundry inside," Lympia said. She pulled out one of the carriers to show them. "The light clothes were in one basket. The darks were in another basket. And I laid the velvet pouch in the bottom of the carrier."

They followed her as she pushed the balloon carrier over to the washtubs. "Then I put Twire's lights in the wash," Lympia went on. "I left the basket by the tubs."

They followed her to the sinks. "Here I scrubbed some of the stains on one of the darks."

They followed her back to the washtubs. "I put Twire's darks in the water. I left the basket in front of the tub while I cleaned them."

They followed her to the balloon-carrier storage area. "Then I brought the balloon carrier back here," said Lympia. She tied up the one she had borrowed again. "And I took a break while the wash was soaking."

Lympia put a hand to her forehead. "I guess I forgot to take the velvet pouch out of the carrier before I returned it," she said sheepishly.

8

LYMPIA HAD NO idea who had used that balloon carrier next. But she did have one more piece to add to the puzzle.

"Yesterday lots of laundry-talent fairies were washing and folding tablecloths for the Queen's Arrival Day party," Lympia remembered. "They loaded all the clean tablecloths and napkins into balloon carriers. Then the celebration-setup fairies came to pick them up." Lympia shrugged. "Maybe one of them took the carrier with the pouch in it – hidden under the clean laundry?" she suggested.

Prilla thanked Lympia for her help. Vidia was already halfway across the room, heading for the door.

"Hey, Vidia! Wait up!" Prilla called as she chased after her.

Vidia waited outside the laundry room for Prilla. "We've been at this all morning!" Vidia fumed. "And we're no closer to finding the crown!"

Prilla smiled. She patted Vidia on the back. "Sure we are," Prilla said encouragingly. "We're hot on the trail! We're putting all the pieces together! We're solving the mystery!" Prilla's blue eyes twinkled. "And you've got to admit – it is kind of fun."

Vidia pursed her lips and squinted at Prilla. Then, without a word, she turned and zipped off down the corridor. But before she did, Prilla thought she saw a tiny twinkle in Vidia's eye, too.

They tracked down the celebration-setup fairies in the tearoom. When they weren't setting up for a big party, they helped the kitchen fairies with the setup of meals. As Prilla and Vidia entered the tearoom, some were setting the tables for lunch. Others were carrying dishes and trays out of the kitchen and placing them on a buffet table.

Prilla's stomach growled. She knew that she might not have the chance to eat for the rest of the afternoon. So she helped herself to a strawberry angel food cupcake from the buffet.

Then, her mouth full, she spotted Vidia already talking to Nora, one of the celebration-setup fairies. Prilla flew over in time to hear Vidia's question.

"Excuse me, honey lamb," said Vidia. She turned on the sweetness. "But did you find a black velvet pouch when you were setting up for the party yesterday? It was mixed in with the tablecloths."

Nora was laying out forks and knives on one table. Without even looking up, she replied, "You mean the velvet pouch with the

149

crown inside it?"

Vidia and Prilla couldn't believe their ears. Did Nora know where the crown was? And if she did, why hadn't she said anything at the emergency meeting?

Vidia spoke first. "Yes! Yes!" she cried. "The one with the crown inside it! Nora, where is it?"

Nora looked up. She was taken aback by the excitement in Vidia's voice. "Well, we took it out of the pouch and threw it in the back room with all the other crowns," she said casually.

Now Vidia and Prilla were *really* confused. "What other crowns?" Prilla asked.

"The crowns for the party," Nora replied. She put the spoons down on the table in a pile. Then she flew away and waved for Vidia and Prilla to follow. "Come on. I'll show you."

Nora led them out of the tearoom and into

the dining hall, where the party would have been the night before. A balloon arch still framed the doorway. The tables were still draped in gold and lacy spiderwebs. Everything was ready for the party that hadn't happened.

In the far corner of the dining hall was a small door marked STOREROOM. Nora flew directly to it and opened the door. Then she stood to one side to let Vidia and Prilla go in first.

The room was dimly lit by natural light from one small window high on the wall. At first, Vidia and Prilla could only just make out the rough outline of items in piles on the floor.

Then, as their eyes adjusted to the light, the forms became clearer.

There before them were stacks and stacks of shiny, glittering crowns – and every one of them looked exactly like Queen Ree's!

9

"They look good – almost real. Don't they?" Nora said proudly. She pointed to the crowns piled in the storeroom.

"What?" Prilla replied. Her head was spinning.

"What do you mean, '*almost real*'?" Vidia asked.

Nora picked up a crown from one of the piles. "Well, they're fakes, of course," she began. "For the Arrival Day party, we had them made to look just like Queen Ree's real crown. Yesterday evening we were going to put one at each seat. Each fairy could wear it during the party and take it home as a party gift!" Nora smiled and put the fake crown on her head. "Good idea, huh?" she added.

Vidia and Prilla said nothing. They just stared at the fake crowns with wide eyes. So

Nora went on.

"But when the Queen announced that the real crown was missing" – Nora shot a quick glance at Vidia – "and the party was called off, we left them here." Nora took the crown off her head. She put it back on a pile. "Now we're not sure what to do with them."

Vidia sighed. "Well," she said, "I'll tell you the first thing to be done with them."

Nora looked at Vidia. "What?" she said.

"We'll need to go through them all and look for the real crown," Vidia replied.

Now Nora looked confused. Prilla explained everything – from Rhia's dropping off the dented crown at Aidan's to Lympia's leaving the crown in the pouch in her balloon carrier.

Nora's eyes widened in shock. "But that means . . . " Her voice trailed off as she put the pieces together. "The crown in the velvet pouch . . . the one we tossed in here . . . "

Prilla and Vidia nodded. Yes, the Queen's real crown – an irreplaceable work of art from the earliest days of Pixie Hollow – was here. It was somewhere in this dark, dusty storeroom.

How in the world would they find it, mixed in with hundreds of fake crowns that looked exactly like it?

"Nora," Prilla said at last, "who made the fake crowns? Who figured how to copy the real thing so well?"

"Dupe," Nora replied. "You know, he's one of the art talents. He spent a lot of time getting it just right."

A short while later, a gloomy Dupe stood in the storeroom, in the middle of piles and piles of crowns. Prilla, Vidia and Nora had just filled him in on the problem.

"Well, I worked so hard trying to make the fake crowns look just like the Queen's," Dupe said to the fairies in a sad tone. "And now we're all wishing I hadn't done such a good job."

Poor Dupe! He *had* worked hard on the crown party gifts. Then the party had been called off. Now it looked as though the crowns might never be used.

But Vidia wasn't in a sympathetic mood. She wasn't looking forward to their task. Sifting through all the fake crowns would be like looking for a needle in a haystack. "So," she said impatiently to Dupe, "is there a way to tell the real crown from the fakes?"

Dupe nodded. "There is," he replied. "But not by looking at them." He picked up a crown. "You see the delicate metalwork? These rows of moonstones? The large fire opal in the centre?" He pointed out all the crown's beautiful features. "When I crafted the fake crowns, I used tin scraps and fake jewels for all of these things. But with a lot of fairy dust and some special magic, I glossed over all the imperfections. There is no way to tell that they aren't real."

The fairies looked carefully at the crown Dupe was holding. It was true. None of them would have guessed that it wasn't the real thing.

But when Dupe said the word 'imperfections', Prilla had an idea. "Wait!" she said. "What about the dent? There was a dent in the real crown that Rhia wanted to have fixed. Can't we just look for the crown with the dent?" Prilla asked Dupe. "That one will be the real one, won't it?"

Dupe shook his head. "I'm afraid not," he said. "I copied the real crown exactly – dent and all." He pointed to a dent on the fake crown he was holding. "Of course, in time the magic will wear off," he went on. "The fake crowns will look like what they really are – just some scraps of metal with hunks of quartz and coloured pebbles stuck onto them."

But that wouldn't happen for months. They needed to find the real crown now!

"There was only one part of the real crown that I wasn't able to copy," Dupe added.

The fairies' faces brightened as Dupe went on.

"When it's placed on someone's head, the real crown magically changes its size to fit the wearer perfectly," he explained. "My magic wasn't strong enough to do that. All of the fake crowns are size five."

As it turned out, none of them had size five heads. Prilla and Nora were both size four.

Dupe was a size six. Vidia was a size three-and-a-half.

At that, Vidia laughed scornfully. "Let me get this straight," she said. "We have to try on all these crowns? Until we find one that magically fits our heads?"

Dupe nodded. "Oh. And one other thing," he said. "There are some words you need to say when you put the crown on your head. The words trigger the real crown's magic."

Vidia eyed him warily. "What kind of words?" she asked. She sounded almost afraid to hear the answer.

Dupe cleared his throat. "You have to say:

> *'Pixie Hollow,*
> *Mother Dove –*
> *The world we cherish,*
> *The one we love'.*"

Vidia cringed in disgust. "Ugh!" she cried. "That's got to be the sappiest thing I've ever heard!"

Prilla clapped Vidia good-naturedly on the back. "Well, Vidia," she said, "it may not roll off the tongue now. But it will in a few hours – after you've said it a *few hundred times*!"

10

At first, Vidia refused to try on any of the crowns. There was no way she was going to say the magic words. Instead, she made herself comfortable on a flour-filled sack in one corner of the storeroom. She sat there stubbornly, with her arms crossed, watching Prilla, Nora and Dupe try on crowns and say the verse.

But before long, Vidia grew impatient – and bored. She realized that the search would move along faster if she helped.

"For goodness' sake," she snapped. "Can't you go any faster? At this rate, we'll be here all night!" She hopped off the flour sack.

Vidia picked up a crown. She placed it on her size-three-and-a-half head. Too large, it slipped down and covered her eyes.

Then, in barely a whisper, Vidia said the

magic words.

> *"Pixie Hollow,*
> *Mother Dove –*
> *The world we cherish,*
> *The one we love."*

It pained her to say those corny lines. To make matters worse, nothing happened. Nothing at all. No change. No magic. The crown remained as ill-fitting as ever.

Vidia sighed, took off the crown and threw it into the fake pile. Then she picked up another crown and tried again.

This went on through the evening and into the night. It was slow going. At midnight, the unsorted piles still towered higher than the fake pile.

Hours later, as the first light of the new day peeked in through the high window, Vidia paused in her search and yawned. She looked around at the others. Dupe was slumped against a box, sound asleep. A crown was perched on his head. Nora's eyes were also closed. She had stretched out on the floor right in the middle of the unsorted crowns.

Prilla, however, kept searching.

Vidia reached for another crown from an unsorted pile. By now, the task was automatic. Reach for crown, place on head, say words, throw. Reach for crown, place on head, say words, throw.

So when it happened, Vidia almost missed it.

Reach for crown, place on head, say words –

But this time, as Vidia reached up to take off the crown, she froze.

Was it her imagination? Or had this crown just . . . shrunk?

When she put this one on, it had slipped down and covered her eyes like all the others. But now, as she reached up to touch it, it sat perfectly on the top of her head.

Slowly, Vidia took the crown off. She held it in front of her and stared at it. So this was it. This was Queen Ree's crown. The real thing. Vidia couldn't help giving a sigh of relief. Now she knew for sure that she couldn't be banished from Pixie Hollow. Not only could she prove, beyond a doubt, that she hadn't taken the crown. But she had also figured out exactly how the crown had gone missing – *and* she had tracked it down, too. Yes, Vidia had cleared her name.

She opened her mouth to tell Prilla – then closed it again. A thought was forming in her mind. Her relief had been so strong at first that it had blocked out other very different feelings. But now those other feelings were coming back: anger, bitterness. And something else, too. What was it? A desire for . . . revenge!

Almost everyone in Pixie Hollow had believed Vidia had taken the crown. Now here it was in her hands. She could do whatever she wanted with it. So why *shouldn't* she go ahead and prove everyone right? Why *shouldn't* she steal it? She could probably steal it *and* get away with it! She could hide it from Prilla, Nora and Dupe. She could show up at her hearing and tell the Queen about their investigation – leaving out the part about how she found the real crown in the storeroom. Everyone else's story would cast enough doubt for Vidia to be found not guilty. And yet, she *would* have the real crown!

Vidia hadn't said a word since she had made her discovery. She also had not taken her eyes off the crown.

Now, finally, she looked up and across the room at Prilla.

To Vidia's surprise, Prilla was staring right at her. In fact, it felt as though Prilla were staring right *through* her.

Prilla knew exactly what was going on in Vidia's head.

***

In the courtyard of the Home Tree, Queen Ree tried to start the hearing.

"Everyone, please!" she shouted over the noise. "Please, quiet down!"

Slowly but surely, the chit-chatting fairies and sparrow men settled down. They had all come to hear what Vidia would say. Just as on the night of the emergency meeting, every spot that was comfortable for sitting – every toadstool and mossy mound – was taken.

Right in front of the Home Tree stood

Queen Ree. A ray of mid-morning sun shone down through the leaves and fell on her like a spotlight. At the Queen's left, Vidia stood with her hands clasped behind her back.

About ten inches from Vidia, Prilla sat on a toadstool in the front row of the crowd and looked on uneasily.

"Vidia?" Queen Ree said. "This hearing is your chance to speak to the charge against you. You have been charged with the theft of the royal crown." The Queen waved Vidia over, letting her take centre stage. "Let us all listen with open hearts and open minds to whatever Vidia says."

Queen Ree took several steps back. Vidia came forward, her hands still clasped behind her back.

"Well," Vidia said in a loud, clear voice, "I really don't have anything to say." She took one hand from behind her back and held it out towards the Queen. In her hand was the crown. "I think this should speak for itself," Vidia added with a wry smile.

A cry of surprise rippled through the crowd.

"So she *did* take it!" Tinker Bell shouted.

"She admits it!" came another cry from somewhere in the crowd.

"Banish her!" someone else shouted.

Queen Ree stepped forward to speak to the crowd. She held her hands up. "Please!" she cried. "You must stay quiet during the hearing. Otherwise, I will have to hold it in private."

Silence settled over the crowd once more. Queen Ree turned to Vidia. She took the crown from Vidia's hand.

"I don't understand," the Queen said. "Don't you want to say anything about where you got this, or why you have it?"

Vidia shook her head. "No," she replied. "But, if it is all right with you, my dear queen" – Vidia smiled sweetly and bowed low before Queen Ree – "I would like to call some others up to say a few words."

The Queen nodded. Vidia looked out into the crowd. "I would like to ask Rhia, Aidan, Twire, Lympia, Nora and Dupe to come up here," she announced.

One by one, the four fairies and two sparrow men flew out of the crowd. Each of them looked somewhat embarrassed as he or she stood next to Vidia.

When all six of them stood facing the crowd, Vidia nodded at Rhia. "Rhia," she said, "be a dear and tell everyone what you did with the crown on the morning of the Arrival Day party."

And so, Rhia began. It was the tale of how the Queen's crown went on a long and eventful journey all over the Home Tree. Timidly, Rhia told her part of the story. She had brought the crown to be fixed, and had misunderstood Aidan's wave.

"If only I hadn't been in such a rush," Rhia moaned.

Aidan picked up the story next. He told everyone that his earplugs had kept him from hearing Rhia. He described how Twire must have picked up the crown along with the scrap metal.

And so on and so on . . . The tale was passed from one storyteller to the next – from Aidan to Twire to Lympia to Nora to Dupe. Each one explained his or her role in the disappearance of the crown.

"So once I explained how to tell the difference between the fake crowns and the real one," Dupe said, wrapping up his part of the story, "we all started trying them on." He shrugged and turned to Vidia. "And eventually, Vidia found it. The Queen's crown."

And that, it seemed, was the end of the story.

Only Vidia and Prilla knew that one part, towards the end, had been left out. It was the part where Vidia had almost become the evil fairy that many in Pixie Hollow already thought she was. It was also the part where she had made a better choice.

Vidia sneaked a sideways glance at Prilla. Prilla smiled at her – and a strange thing happened. Vidia smiled back at Prilla. It wasn't one of Vidia's fake, sickly sweet smiles, either. It was a real, true sign of Vidia's gratitude for Prilla's help. Prilla knew there would be no thank you. She knew that, from this moment on, she and Vidia would probably never speak of the matter again. She knew that the smile was all she would get.

But it was enough.

Queen Ree stepped forward to speak to everyone. "Well," she said, "I think that clears the matter up for me. I have no doubt that everyone here feels the same." She glanced around at the crowd. Everyone nodded in agreement.

"There's just one other thing," the Queen went on. She stepped over to Vidia's side and laid a hand on her shoulder. "Vidia, I owe you an apology," she said. "We all owe you an apology. We accused you of something you did not do. We also owe you our thanks. You worked hard to find the crown and return it safely." Queen Ree turned to face the crowd. "To celebrate, I'd like to reschedule the party."

The crowd cheered.

"Only, this party will not be an Arrival Day celebration for me," the Queen went on.

"It will be a party for Vidia, too." She looked questioningly at Vidia. "Will you be our guest of honour?" the Queen asked.

Vidia smiled. "Really, Ree, you flatter me," she said. Her voice dripped with sarcasm. "But, frankly, I'd rather go on another wild-goose chase around the Home Tree, searching for one of your missing baubles, than come to any party of yours." She smiled and took off into the air.

Almost as one, the crowd gasped in shock at Vidia's rudeness. To say such a thing – when the Queen had been trying to make everything better!

But then again, Vidia had never been one to mince words.